A JEALOUS TYPE OF LOVE

By: Bri Deshai

FOLLOW ME ON SOCIAL MEDIA

Instagram: @brideshai

Snapchat: _briiiida

Facebook: @Bri Deshai

For sneak peeks, release dates, and cover reveals, make sure to join my reading group on Facebook @Bri's beauties Reading group. Also make sure yo go and like my fan page Author-BriDeshai!

CHAPTER 1

Pooh

"Ahmad stop fucking playing before you drop me," I laughed while trying to get out of his reach. Ahmad and I have been together for three years now, and he is the love of my life. When I laid eyes on him, I was pretty sure I laid eyes on an Angel. Even till this day, he's nothing but eye candy. He stands at about six foot four, with creamy colored skin, his piercing hazel eyes is what caught my attention. He was the perfect man, charming, loving, he guarded me with his heart and needless to say he was the missing puzzle piece to my heart, and now we were expecting twins, I couldn't imagine life without him.

"Stop fucking crying all the time, now move so I can get ready for work," he sat me down on the bed and kissed my cheek.

"Being in the streets all day with my brother is not considered work Ahmad," he shook his head and walked in the bathroom. He was trying to avoid the conversation that we have every morning. Ahmad runs an illegal business with my three brothers and my best friend. I hate the fact that he decided to get back in the drug game after we lost our first child, but it's something that I must deal with I guess because obviously nothing is changing any time soon.

"Ahmad stop trying to avoid the conversation, you know I don't want you in the streets anymore," I yelled while walking into the bathroom.

"What did I tell you about yelling Bianca? I'm not trying to hear all of that right now. Go lay yo ass back down so I can take a shower without you nagging." He said in a dismissive tone. Me being the stubborn one I sat on the toilet and waited until he got out of the shower. When Ahmad says that he is done talking about a situation its best if you let it go because he has a temper out of this world. I love Ahmad with everything in me but sometimes I can't deal with his anger.

"Pooh where yo fat ass at?" I heard my brother Kj yell while probably going through my refrigerator. My brother Ka'Mari or Kj was not only my brother, but he was my best friend. Our relationship was kind of bittersweet though, it was sweet because I could tell my brother everything and we don't keep secrets from each other but it's bitter because he still treats me like I'm still thirteen years old, he also gets in me and Ahmad's relationship. Every time we fuss or fight, he's the first one over here. I walked out of the bathroom, walked over to the closet so I could slip on some of Ahmad's sweats, and I made my way downstairs to the kitchen. Just like I figured Kj was standing in the refrigerator getting stuff to make a sandwich.

"Every time you come over here, you're always in my refrigerator," I said while walking over to the Cabinet and pulling out the bread.

"Well maybe if you move back in with me, I wouldn't be here all of the time. Where is Ahmad at, we gone be late to our meeting cause his ass is taking forever," He mushed me in the back of my head, grabbed his sandwich and walked to the living room. I just shook my head and cleaned up the mess that he left. After I was done in the kitchen, I walked in the living room and sat on Kj's lap.

"Yo ass getting too big to be sitting on my fucking lap Pooh, we need to talk real quick."

"About what Ka'Mari, what did you do?" Every time Kj

says that he needs to talk its always something that he needs me to fix.

"Man chill I ain't did shit, but you remember the guy who used to work with Pops?"

"Of course I do, what's wrong with Uncle, is he okay?" Before my daddy adopted me when I was twelve him, my Uncle D, my biological father, use to be drug lords. They were the most respected men in the entire world, but that changed when my parents and my father's brother got killed. My Uncle D moved away because he couldn't stand to stay in Atlanta without my father.

"Him and his family are moving back here, and he wanted his two sons to be in the family business. I know who they are because we always kept in touch with each other, but you don't so I want you to meet them today."

"Um okay, but what do me meeting them have to do with them being in the streets with yall?" I didn't have a say so in who could run the family business, because if it was up to me nobody would be out there selling drugs.

"I just want you to get to know them Pooh that's it. Are you cooking tonight?"

"Carter already called and said he wanted Chili so that's for dinners," When I said that he mugged the fuck out of me which cause me to laugh. Carter was Kj's right hand man, and my best friend in the entire world. Me and Carter have been best friends for about four years now, and just like me Carter was adopted into the family, but the only difference was Carter was accepted into the family. The more I was around Carter the closer we got, now I couldn't get rid of his ignorant ass.

"What yall niggas down here talking about, and why the fuck do you have my sweats on?" Ahmad said walking down the stairs looking like a snack. He had on a Nike shirt, black joggers, and his slides. He snatched me from Kj's lap and wrapped his arms around me. Even though I was still mad at him just being wrapped up in his arms makes my heart melt.

"Nigga what took yo ass so fucking long? We already late to our meeting and you wanna come down here and start fucking with her fat ass, bring yo ass on," Ahmad's crazy ass busted out laughing which caused me to laugh. Kj hates being late for anything, that's why I'm trying to figure out why did he decide to ride with Ahmad's late ass.

"Bro shut yo cry baby ass up and come on, how are we gone be late to our own meeting?"

"Nigga shut yo ass up, you know I hate being late to shit," Kj got up and walked out the door. Ahmad's petty ass sat down on the couch and started to roll up a blunt. He likes making people mad I swear.

"Stop pissing my brother off Ahmad that shit ain't funny, you know he hates being late," I sat in his lap and kissed his juicy fat lips.

"Come on baby you see me trying to roll this shit up, I need to get high cause yo brother gone piss me off."

"Yall argue like two bitches, what time are you coming back?"

"I don't know why?"

"Can you bring me back a rib platter and 3 slices of turtle cheesecake, oh and a large Strawberry milkshake?" I laid my head on his shoulder and put his hand across my belly trying to butter him up. Ahmad hates when I eat unhealthy stuff, but he knows that I get what I want so I knew that he was going to give in. He started rubbing my belly which caused the twins to go crazy.

"You know I'm not getting you that shit Bianca, you don't need any of that, I'll bring you back a grilled chicken sandwich." I frown just thinking about healthy food.

"Baby please I won't ask you for anything else, and I'll give you some sloppy head tonight," he looked at me and busted out laughing.

"Stop playing with me shorty, I was gone get that any way. Get up and walk me to the door," I got up and followed him to the car. I wrapped my hand around his neck and looked at him.

"Be careful baby, you too Kj," He looked out the window and nodded, Ahmad pecked my lips and rubbed my belly.

"Always ma, now give me one more kiss so I can leave," I kissed him passionately and let go of him.

"Now take yo ass in the house, I love you."

"I love you too baby, please be careful and call me every ten minutes please," he chuckled and got in the car.

"Nigga don't forget my food either," He rolled down the window and flipped me off, I just laughed and walked back in the house. I love that man with everything in me.

CHAPTER 2

Ahmad

"Kj would you please shut the fuck damn, if you wanted to be on time, then you know damn well you shouldn't have agreed to pick me up in the first fucking place. I should've rolled another blunt fucking with yo annoying ass," ever since we been in this damn car Kj haven't done anything but bitch and it was starting to piss me off. I have been cool with Kj and his family ever since we were in middle school together. Kj and his brothers were getting their ass kicked by some bitches and I had to help them because they were looking pathetic, ever since then we have been close, well except for Kj and I. Our friendship kind of drifted when I started dating Pooh, when he found out about us three years ago, he made Pooh move back in with him, but of course, that didn't stop her from coming to see me, and eventually Kj got used to it. That didn't mean he liked the idea he just accepted the fact that his sister loves the kid.

"Ahmad shut the fuck up and get out of my fucking car before I beat yo ass," when I looked around and realized that we made it to the warehouse, I quickly got my ass out of the car and made my way inside. As soon as I opened the doors, everybody looked at me like they wanted to kill me.

"My nigga can you ever be on time?" Carter said while I sat down next to him, I snatched the blunt out of his hands, leaned back in the chair and took a pull from the blunt.

"I could but I don't like looking at y'all niggas all day."

"Fuck you nigga, where is Kj at?" I pointed towards the door and Kj was walking in with his Uncle's kids.

"Sorry I'm late, obviously Ahmad doesn't know the definition of a damn clock," Kj mugged me and sat at the front of the table.

"Nigga shut yo bitch ass up and just start the damn meeting," Kj smacked me in the back of my head and started talking.

"Alright, so the reason why I called this meeting is because I want everybody to get to know your new bosses Killa and Davon. They will oversee the shipment and making sure that everything is alright, and yall niggas ain't fucking up. If y'all have any questions or concerns they will be your point of contact for now on, does anybody have any questions?" We all looked around and made sure that none of our workers didn't have any questions. When nobody spoke up, I stood up and walked towards the front of our warehouse and spoke.

"Tony what's been going on man?" I asked one of our workers, Tony looked at me with a confused look on his face.

"Whhat what you mean Ahmad?" He stuttered over his words.

"Shit you tell me? We been trying to figure out why have yo trap been the only one short $5,000. What the fuck is up?" Tony looked at all of us and held his head down.

"Alright y'all this meeting is over, I will call everybody in like a week so yall can come and reup, everybody get the fuck out except for Tony," I said continuing to look at Tony.

"So, Tony what's been going on man, why have you been stealing from us?"

"I'm sorry man, I just needed some help with my mother. We just found out that she has kidney failure and I needed some extra money to cover her medical bill," Tony admitted.

"Nigga all you had to do was tell us, you know we look out for each other around here, you fucked up man." Carter shook his head and shot Tony between the eyes. Tony was one of our solid members, so it fucked me up to watch him steal from us. I looked around the room and notice everybody had the same somber look on their face, I couldn't stand looking at Tony's lifeless body anymore, I got up and walked out of the door. When I made it outside, I pulled my phone our and Facetimed Pooh. As soon as she answered the phone, she had a mug on her face.

"Why the fuck are you looking like that bae?"

"Because I told you to call me every ten minutes, and it's been about two or three hours," I laughed cause her ass was real life pouting. My baby was so fucking beautiful, her perfect Mocha skin complexion was a perfect match with her luscious curves, her brown eyes, five-foot frame, and soft pouty lips drove me insane. Even though my baby was plus size, she carried it well. That's another thing that I love about her, she doesn't let her size control her, she was perfect in my eyes.

"If you don't stop all that pouting, you know I was not about to call your spoiled ass every ten minutes. What are you doing anyways?"

"Well I was about to go to sleep, but I guess I'll just stay up and wait for you to come home with my rib platter," I wish she would forget about this damn rib platter.

"I'm about to go get it now with yo fat ass, I think yo brother and Carter were coming to the house tonight."

"I know that's why I need one of y'all to go to the store for me, I need some stuff to make Chili tonight."

"Carter's ass needs to go since he is the one that wanted chili tonight, I'm yo man but Carter gets to choose what we eat for dinner, please help me understand that," The only thing she could do was laugh because she knows I was right. She spoils

Carter, and that shit irritated me to the fullest. That's another reason why I don't really fuck with her family like that. I feel like she always put them before me and that shit really pisses me off.

"Nigga will you stop cup caking and bring yo ass over here," her older brother Kenyon said. Kenyon was the joker of the group, he was the type of person to talk mad shit to you but beat yo ass in the same breath. I think that nigga is real life crazy. I walked over to where everybody was and continued to talk to my wife.

"Ask yo brothers to go to the store for you, I have to go to Papa Jay to get yo ribs."

"Forget the food just hurry home, I want you before my brothers get here," reading between the lines I understood exactly what she was saying.

"Alright let me finish talking to these niggas and I will be home to bless yo ass with this dick in about fifteen minutes." She blushed and nodded her head. I hung up the phone and focused on these niggas.

"Yo Ahmad these are my boys Killa and Davon, this is my annoying ass brother, and Pooh's boyfriend, Ahmad," I looked at them and just nodded my head. I don't have anything against them, I'm just not fond of meeting new people. That nigga Killa just laughed and walked away.

"Damn Ahmad why you act like this nigga just stole yo last cookie?" Kenyon said laughing.

"'Shut the fuck up Kenyon, I don't have anything against them I just don't know them and Pooh said one of yall needs to go to the store to get some shit to make Chili." I said then walked away. I didn't have time to deal with these childish ass niggas, my baby wants me home, so she can get some dick.

• •

"Baby wake up and get yo damn phone please," I quickly got up and picked up my phone before Pooh started acting crazy. She hates when people mess with her while she sleeps, her ass will literally cuss somebody out if they wake her up. I looked at my phone and it was this hoe that I fuck from time to time.

Heather: Hey daddy where have you been? I miss you

Me: What the fuck did I tell you about texting my phone and shit Heather damn.

Heather: I'm sorry baby we miss you.

I looked at the picture she sent me, and it was her freshly shaved pussy, I quickly deleted the picture and turned my phone off. I know I'm wrong for cheating on Bianca, but I'm a man and I have my needs. I never wanted to hurt her but sometimes she gets on my fucking nerves and I need a break from her. If she ever finds out and think she is about to leave me I will kill her. When I looked at her and noticed that she was knocked out, I decided to fuck with her, I pulled her close to me and kissed her passionately.

"Ahmad please stop touching me, go find somebody else to fuck with damn."

"If you weren't pregnant with my baby, I would push yo ass out of this bed."

"Ahmad please go find somebody to play with," She cried and tried to roll over, but I had a strong grip around her waist.

"I wanna play with you baby wake yo ass up."

"Ahmad stop tickling me, you gone make me pee on myself," I place my hand on her stomach and on cue my boys started kicking like crazy. The bond that I have with my boys is amazing and they are not even here yet.

"Baby stop they be kicking me in my ribs, come on let's go downstairs." She got up put on some shorts and went downstairs to fuck with her brothers. I picked my phone back up, turned it on and called Heather back.

"I knew you was gone call me, what's up daddy?"

"Bitch don't fucking what's up me, what the fuck did I tell you about calling me when I'm around my wife?"

"I don't understand you Ahmad, when you're with me, you're telling me how much you hate being with her, and you that you were going to break up with her, so we can be together. Why are you doing this to me Ahmad I love you," I ran my hand across my head and closed my eyes. The only reason why I told her that was because she was threating to tell Pooh about us and I couldn't lose her.

"Listen baby you have to give me time okay, she is pregnant with my babies, and I work with her brothers. All I need is time is that okay with you?"

"I guess Ahmad, but you have to tell her, I'm tired of being treated like a hoe."

"I you baby, now get that pussy ready for daddy I'll be over there in a minute," I heard a knock at the door and quickly hung up the phone. Pooh's best friend Ash walked in the door and looked at me.

"Who were you just on the phone with?"

"Ashton if you don't get the fuck out of my room, what the fuck do you want?" Her ghetto ass popped her lip and rolled her eyes.

"I was looking for Pooh but obviously she's not up here."

"Ash please get the fuck out of my room, Bianca is probably in the basement with her brothers."

"We need to talk Ahmad," I just got up and walked in the bathroom. Before Pooh and I decided to be together me and Ash fucked around heavy behind Bianca's back. We knew what we were doing was wrong but for some reason I couldn't get enough of Ash, well that's until her dumb ass ended up pregnant. She told Pooh that her baby daddy was somebody that she met in the club. When Ash found out that I was not about to take care of the baby she sent her away to live with her family in New York. Till this day Pooh doesn't know what truly happened and I don't plan on tell her either. When I made it out of the bathroom, Ash was gone. I walked downstairs and didn't see my wife anywhere.

"Yo Kj where Pooh at?"

"Downstairs talking to Ash, yo we got a problem, Killa said he got a call from one of our workers," he stopped talking and ate a spoon full of chili that my baby cooked earlier. I hate when his greedy ass does that.

"Kj what the fuck is the problem."

"Chill nigga, he got a call from Rock saying that an unmark car has been following him. He said when he pulled up to the warehouse the car just drove off."

"Man, what the fuck bro, why didn't his ass call us when he was getting followed?" That shit just pissed me off.

"That's what I said, but you know that Rock is a solid dude, I'm on my way to the warehouse now."

"I'm going with you, just let me tell Pooh really quick," I walked downstairs to the basement and Pooh, and Ash were on the couch laughing.

"'Baby come here real quick," She looked at me and frowned.

"Bianca bring yo ass over here, before I beat yo ass my nigga, I'm not in the mood to deal with you right now," I felt my temper rising and her ass wasn't making it any better. She quickly got up and walked over to me.

"What do you want?"

"Bianca don't fucking play with me, what is wrong with you?"

"Who were you on the phone with?" I looked at Ash and

she had a smirk on her face.

"I was on the phone with my mama baby, I'm about to go with Kj to handle some business I'll be back," I pulled her towards me and forced her to kiss me. I went upstairs and walked out the door, Ash was starting shit and I had to nip that in the bud quick.

CHAPTER 3

Pooh

"**A**sh are you sure you heard him on the phone with another woman?" For some reason I couldn't see Ahmad cheating on me, I was Ahmad's everything, and if he wasn't in the house with me, he was running the streets with my brother.

"Yes, I'm sure boo, when I went upstairs looking for you, I heard him on the phone with some girl, would I lie to you?" I looked at her like she was dumb, Ash and I have been best friends since we were kids. My biological parents adopted her when we were only five years old, so we were more like sisters then best friends. For some reason Her and Ahmad never liked each other, it's like every time they are around each other they argue.

"Well I'll talk to him about it later I doubt that it was anything serious, I'm about to go upstairs and watch Netflix, are you coming?" She looked at me then rolled her eyes.

"Nah I think I'm going to go home I have a busy day tomorrow."

"Bitch what do you have to do, you don't have a job, but whatever lock my door on your way out," I rolled my eyes and walked back upstairs. I don't have time for Ash and her nasty attitude. I walked in my kitchen, grabbed a bag of chips, and made my way into the living room. As soon as I stepped foot in the room, I seen who I'm guessing is one of my uncle's kids. When Ahmad made it home, he fucked me silly which cause me to fall asleep, so I didn't even know that my brothers were here, and I'm kind of confused as to why he's still here when my brothers are gone. I sat on the couch across from him and turned Netflix on, I was trying to ignore him, but I couldn't. This man is so freaking fine! He looked to be about six three, his beautiful cream skin complexion matched perfectly with his brown eyes and deep waves. I have never seen a man so beautiful in my life, don't get me wrong Ahmad is gorgeous, but this nigga right here... Is a fucking God.

"Why the fucking is you staring at me like that?" He asked with a mug on his face. Not realizing I was staring, I quickly turned away and focused on the tv.

"So, you don't hear me talking to you?" Once again, I tried to ignore him, but when he got up and sat by me, I froze. Even being close to him sent chills through my body. I had to get myself together, because Ahmad would kill me if he even thought I was getting next to another man.

"I'm just trying to figure out why you are here and didn't go with my brothers?" He chuckled and snatched the remote from me.

"Get yo ass out of my house now!" I turned the TV off walked to the door and opened it. The way he looked at me had me wanting to run, it was a look that made you feel like you were about to get in trouble with yo daddy. He stood by me closed the door and said.

"Sit yo crazy ass down, I don't feel like playing games with you." The way those words flowed out of his mouth had me wanting to jump on him and fuck him right here, right now. I sat down but made sure I sat far away from him.

"What's your real name?" I asked I'm not about to sit here and call this man Killa, that shit sounds crazy as fuck.

"Oh, now yo mean ass wanna talk," He said getting smart like he wasn't in my shit.

"Nigga excuse me? If you haven't realized you're in my

shit, so I suggest you pipe down before we have a problem," Again, this nigga chuckled and turned the tv back on. I don't even let Ahmad talk to me like that, but I ain't gone lie I like that aggressive shit. I picked up my phone and dialed Kj's number, but when he didn't answer I decided to call my other brother Kayin.

"What do you need sis, we're busy?" His rude ass said as soon as he picked up the phone. Kayin is not exactly a people's person. he is very rude, mean and disrespectful. That's why he has never been in a relationship because he doesn't know how to talk to people.

"Don't talk to me like that Kayin, I was trying to call Kj but when he didn't answer I decided on you."

"What the fuck do yo fat ass want Bianca? I told you that we were busy."

"Why did yall leave this disrespectful nigga here?"

"Man, because we needed somebody there to watch you, and before you start, I know you're grown but you're also pregnant with my nephews and I'll be damn if something happens to yall," I automatically started to worry, because the last time they had somebody watch me my daughter got killed.

"Kayin what's going on? Are yall okay?"

"Yes, Pooh we are okay so stop worrying, and chill the fuck out. Killa ain't disrespectful he just doesn't take no shit, so watch what the fuck you say to him," when looked at Killa and he was staring at me with a smirk on his face. I just rolled my eyes and hung up my phone.

"I see yo spoiled ass didn't get what you wanted huh?" I sat back on the couch and smacked my lips.

"Nigga shut yo ass up, you will not disrespect me in my house, do you understand?" He opened his mouth to respond but his phone started ringing. He reached in his pocket, pulled his phone out and answered it.

A JEALOUS TYPE OF LOVE

"What's up Sheila, WHAT, what hospital? I'm on my way. Bitch if something happened to my daughter, I'm going to beat your ass!" He hung up and was walking out of the door.

"I'm going with you," I don't know why I said that, But I felt like l should go. I felt like I needed to be here with him.
• •

The car ride to the hospital was silent, I didn't say anything to him because I felt like he needed to get his head together.

"You go in and I will park your car," I said as soon as we made it to the hospital. He barely stopped the car before he got out, I slid to the driver seat and parked the car, then walked into the hospital.

"Bitch what do you mean you thought she was sleep, she is a fucking kid Sheila!" I walked in and saw security holding him back. I looked across the room and seen my brother's, Ahmad, and I'm guessing Killa's brother Davon.

"Just what I said I thought she was sleep; I didn't know she was up, and her bad ass shouldn't have been in the kitchen anyways," when she said that Davon and Kj ran in and held him back, Ahmad walked over towards me and wrapped his arms around my waist.

"That bitch is about to get her ass beat," He said then kissed me cheek. Her boyfriend got out of the chair he was sitting in, walked over to Killa and got in his face.

"Nigga if I ever see you in my girls face again, I will beat your ass, she already told you she didn't know her daughter was up," Killa smirked tilted his head to the side and punched him right in his face. Everybody was trying to calm him down but failed, even his mama couldn't get him to calm down.

"Baby let me go try to calm him down okay?" Ahmad looked at me strange and let me go.

"Ahmad it's not like that I promise, but I know and everybody else in here know that he needs to calm down, so he can

19

see his child, you remember how that felt right?" He kissed my cheek and followed me to where Killa was. I walked over to Killa and looked him in his eyes. When I touched his chest his looked down at me like he wanted to kill me, but I ignored the looked and continued to try to calm him down

"Not right now, now is not the time, come sit by me and let's wait on the doctors to come out and let us know what's going on with your baby." He looked down at me ran his hands over his head and went to sit down where I was sitting. Kj, Kayin, and Ahmad looked at me like they wanted to kill me, I already knew what he was thinking, and I was gone have to deal with that later. I just sat back down and rubbed Killa's back, I looked at Sheila and this bitch was staring at me like I just stole her man.

"The family of Davonna Lowe" The doctor said while coming towards us. Killa and his baby mama got up at the same time

"Davonna is going to be fine Her scars were not severe, they will completely heal, but she does have second degree burns on her back and chest. She is going to have to use this cream until the burns heal," the doctor said getting straight to the point. When I heard that I instantly got pissed, what kind of mother doesn't watch their child?

"Can I see her?" Killa asked while trying to keep his cool.

"Yes, but she can only have 2 visitors," Killa and his baby mama went back there. I looked up and saw Kj, Kayin, Ahmad, and Kenyon walking towards me.

"Care to explain what the fuck I just saw?" Kj said while standing over me. I looked at them and rolled my eyes.

"First of all, I don't have to explain shit cause what you saw was nothing. I was being there for a fucking friend, his daughter is in the fucking hospital and I know exactly how that feel, and you should to Ahmad. Nothing is going on with me and Killa I can promise you that, I just met dude, but here yall are in my face questioning me on some shit that any human being would do. Fuck outta my face with this bullshit man," I tried to walk away but Ahmad grabbed my arm which caused my brothers to automatically react.

"Yo Ahmad I understand that you're upset but you got about five seconds to get yo fucking hands off my damn sister my nigga," Kenyon said snatching me away from him.

"Kenyon shut yo ass up my nigga. This is my bitch, and I- "

"Nigga watch that Bitch word when you're talking about my sister. I'm not Kj or Kenyon I will beat yo ass and not think twice about it," Kayin pulled out his gun and got in his face. I quickly got in front of the gun and pushed Ahmad back. I looked in his eyes and I could see him slowly blacking out.

"Ahmad please calm down, let's not do this yall please put the guns up," Ahmad looked at me then pushed me out the way.

"Move Pooh these niggas pulled a gun out on me like they gone do something, pulled the trigger nigga," Ahmad walked up to Kayin and got in his face. Kenyon dumb ass busted out laughing.

"Yall look like some straight bitches right now, Davon, you see this shit? Put that gun up nigga that's our fucking brother, regardless of what's going on between him and Pooh we are still brothers at the end of the day. Everybody knows that Bianca ass ain't cheating on Ahmad, I'm about to go back to the warehouse with Carter cause yall niggas are tripping," Kenyon kissed my cheek then walked out. I looked at Kayin and walked over to him.

"Put the fucking gun down Kayin damn, y'all mother fuckers about to give me a damn heart attack." Kayin put the gun down and walked out with Kj.

"Yo ass better not be fucking him, I will kill you, and that nigga, do you hear me Bianca?" I walked over to him and wrapped my arms around his waist.

"You're so sexy when you're jealous, and you know I love you daddy, this pussy only gets wet for you," I kissed his lips and smiled.

"Yea ah ight you heard what the fuck I said, I'm about to go back to the warehouse to finish up this shit, do you need anything?"

"Nope, I will meet you at the house daddy," I pecked his lips one more time and sat down in the chair. I was not leaving until I knew that the baby was okay

"Yo shorty wake up," when I opened my eyes and Killa was sitting by me running his fingers through my hair. That shit felt so good, I'm gone have to tell Ahmad to start doing this.

"Hey, is the baby okay?" I asked quickly which caused him to chuckle.

"yes, she is okay my mama is in there with her now, I can take you home," I frowned at him.

"I'm not going anywhere, I'm fine"

"Good cause I didn't want you to leave," I just laughed and rubbed my stomach.

"I wanna beat yo baby mama's ass, where did her unfit ass go anyway?"

"Calm yo ass down, yo brothers, and yo nigga would kill me if anything happened to you or the babies. Her trifling ass went home cause her nigga said he was tired of being here, what kind of bitch would choose a nigga before her on fucking child?

"wow, that's crazy," we both got quiet and he started running his fingers through my hair again which caused me to start drifting back to sleep.

"Devin"

"Hmm," I asked clearing my throat. I looked at him confused

"That's my name, Devin," he said while looking down at

me and kissing my forehead. Lord I need to get my mind right. I haven't spent a whole twenty-four hours with this nigga, and he is making me forget all about me practically being married.

"Oh, that's cute!" He laughed and playfully mushed my head

"Man don't call my name cute, I'm a real nigga," I just started laughing. We continued to talk the rest of the night.
• •
"Oh, shit Ahmad is going to kill me!" I said while getting up out of the chair I was in. After talking half of the night, we decided to go back into Devin's daughter room, Vonna was the sweetest, and cutest little girl ever. After she warmed up to me, she stayed up and played with me until she wore herself out.

"What time is it?" Devin asked while stretching.

"Six in the morning, I have to get home to my boyfriend, call me when she wakes up, so I can talk to her," I walked over to Vonna, kissed her chunky cheeks and walked out the door. When I stepped outside, I seen Ahmad's car parked besides Dev's car.

"Lord please don't let this man beat my ass." Sighing I walked over to the car and opened the door. He was leaning back in his seat smoking a blunt.

"Baby I'm so sorry, I didn't mean to stay here that long, I was playing and talking to his daughter, and I lost track of time." He started up the car and didn't say anything. I touched his hand, but he quickly moved it away.

"Don't touch me right now Bianca. I'm really trying my hardest not to put my hands on you, and that's only because you're pregnant with my seeds. Sit yo ass back and don't say shit to me," fighting back the tears I nodded my head and was quiet the rest of the way home. Once we made it to the house Ahmad got out the car without even helping me out. I got out the car and slowly walked in the house. I went straight upstairs and stripped out of my clothes. Once I was in the bathroom, I saw that Ahmad was already in the shower, so I slipped in and quickly washed up, so I wouldn't be around him long. I got out the shower, dried myself off and just got in bed without bothering to put clothes on. I saw Ahmad's phone ringing, so I reached over to see who it was.

"Who the fuck is Heather? Hello?"

"Oh, um hey is Ahmad available?"

"He's in the shower, I'm his fiancé can I help you with something?" The girl was silent and then she burst out laughing.

"You can just tell him to use his key to get in, and make sure that he gets our food."

"I will make sure I tell him, Have a good night." I hung up the phone and sat his phone down. I can't believe this nigga is actually cheating on me, then he has the nerve to have this bitch number saved in his phone. Knowing that he is going to be in the shower a while longer I quickly got his phone and went through his messages. This nigga was telling her that he was going to leave me, and the only reason why he is still with me is because of my kids. I heard him turn the shower of, so I quickly sat his phone down, and turned on the tv. He walked out of the shower in a towel and went straight to the closet.

"You want something to eat?" He asked me never looking at me. It was taking a lot for me not to go over there and just cut his nasty ass dick off.

"Nah I'm not hungry, if I do get hungry, I'll just fix me something to eat."

"Coo, I'm about to head out, don't wait up."

"But it's eight in the morning Ahmad, where are you going," he ignored my question and walked out of the door, I 1quickly got up threw on some clothes, and packed an overnight bag. I be damn if I stay here and let this nigga cheat on me, he got me fucked up. Not once have I ever thought about being with another man since we have been together. I love Ahmad too much to do something like that to him. I grabbed my bag and made my way to the garage. I put my things in the back seat, and pulled out my phone to call Ash, but I changed my mind and called Carter. I didn't have time to deal with Ash and her sarcastic ass attitude.

"What's up best friend?"

"Carter can I come stay with you for a while?" He was silent for a moment then he burst out laughing but stopped when he noticed that I wasn't laughing.

"Oh, wait you're serious."

"Yes, Carter I am."

"You know you can stay with me, I'm not there right now but you got a key, I should be there tonight though."

"Okay thank you. I'll text you when I get to your house, love you bye," I hung up the phone and drove to Carters house. Never in a million years would I have thought that Ahmad was cheating on me, but I guess I'm wrong.

CHAPTER 4

Killa

"Daddy I don't wanna go home with mommy, I wanna go with you!" It was taking a lot in me not to leave this hospital and go find Sheila's dumb ass.

"Baby you're going with me, but I need you to calm down okay?" She wiped her face then nodded her head.

"Where did Pooh go daddy?"

"She had to go home but she promised that she will be back, do you want to call her?"

"Yes please," I pulled out my phone and dialed her number.

"Hello?" She answered with an attitude on the fifth ring. Before I could say anything to her Vonna beat me to it.

"POOH!" The excitement in her voice caused Pooh to chuckle.

"Hey chunks! How are you feeling?"

"I would be better if you were up here," me and Pooh started laughing.

"Little girl are you sure that you're three?"

"I AM I AM!"

"Okay okay I'll be up there in thirty minutes okay?"

"YAYYYY!" I laughed and took her off of speaker.

"I promise I didn't put her up to this."

"You probably did but it's okay, I miss her already. I'll be up there shortly with breakfast," she hung up before I could re-

spond. I couldn't say that I wasn't happy. Honestly, I was happy that she was coming back. For some reason being around her calm me down. Even though she is pregnant and damn near married. I just knew I had to have her.
• •

"What are you over there thinking about baby?" My mama asked. I looked at her and smiled.

"You act like you know me old woman." She smiled.

"You're thinking about that Bianca, aren't you?" I just looked away from her and tried not to smile. Pooh came at the exact same time that my mother did, and she decided to wait in the waiting room until my mom left. Pooh was on my mind heavy, the fact that she decided to come back, and she stayed with me last night made me look at her totally different. She wasn't the same spoiled brat that I met, she was actually sweet, but rude at the same time. That's what made me want her sexy ass.

"Gone ma, I'm not playing with you today," she looked at me and chuckled.

"I actually like her, even though she is pregnant and in a relationship with somebody that you work with, but I'll leave you alon...."She didn't get to finish her sentence because Pooh walked in looking all thick and shit.

"Excuse me, I'm sorry to interrupt but I got bored in the waiting room, I can go back if I was interrupting you guys," Pooh said while walking in. My mom looked at her and smiled.

"Oh no baby you're fine, I was about to leave, call me Devin, and Pooh yo Uncle said you need to bring yo hot ass to the house so he can see you," Pooh laughed and hugged my mom.

"Yes, ma'am I'll actually stop by today." My mom walked over kissed my daughter and left.

"Your mom is so freaking pretty," Pooh said as she sat in the chair by Vonna.

"I know, are you gone stay all night?" I asked hoping she is going to say yes.

"Are you trying to get rid of me?" She smirked

"Nah ma, I just wanna make sure you're comfortable, and I know yo nigga gone be tripping if you don't come home," when I said something about Ahmad the smile she was wearing turned into a frown.

"Oh, shit what did that nigga do, did I get you in trouble?"

"No, you didn't, but let's not talk about him right now."

"You are so fucking beautiful," she looked at me then blushed.

"Stop acting so shy, calm down and talk to Daddy," she looked up from her phone and busted out laughing. That's another thing I found out about her, she was so fucking goofy.

"Nigga something is wrong with you; I'm not shy I just don't know what to talk about," I was about to respond but Vonna woke up and started screaming. The doctor a walked in and made sure she was okay, I picked her up she relaxed but she was still crying. This is the shit that I can't take, I hate seeing my baby in pain.

"Give her here," Vonna automatically went to her and laid her head on Pooh's chest. She was still crying but when pooh started singing she calmed down and was playing with Pooh's earrings. She had the voice of an angel. She just keeps amazing me. I had to have this girl.

"You can sing yo ass off Pooh, that shit calmed me down," She shook her head and laughed.

"I used to sing to my daughter all the time it used to calm her down," she started to cry but quickly wiped it away. I was about to ask her about what happened, but I didn't think she wanted to talk about it, so I let it go for now.

"Hello, my name is Janice, and I'm from DFS," I got up

and shook her hand. These nosey ass mother fuckers were going to be in my business now.

"Hello, I'm Devin, Davonna's father, and this is...."

"Bianca I'm a friend," She got up and shook her hand.

"Well hello pretty lady, you must be Davonna." Vonna looked at her and turned her head.

"I'm sorry about that, she isn't feeling well, she's usually so talkative," I said so the social worker. She nodded her head and bent down so she was looking at Vonna.

"Oh no it's okay, I'm here because I heard she had to be rushed to the emergency room."

"Yes ma'am," I said not knowing what to say next.

"Well I'm going to have to ask her a few questions"

"That's fine," Janice reached for Vonna, but she held on tight to Pooh's hand.

"Can I ask you some questions pretty lady?" Vonna looked at me for approval, and I nodded.

"My mommy told me to go in my room cause the scary man was coming over, I told her that I was hungry, and she told me to fix myself something to eat so I went to the kitchen to get something.... I didn't touch the oven daddy I promise," she started crying and ran to me. Seeing my daughter so hurt and crying had me on the verge of blacking out. Sheila's bitch ass better stay the fuck out of my life or I was gone kill her ass. Me and Sheila was never in a relationship, she was just a hoe that I got pregnant because of a drunken night. I clenched my jaw and kissed Vonna on the cheek, I couldn't even speak. I guess Pooh felt my tension because she came down over, and bent down in front of Vonna, and looked at her.

"It's okay baby, you're not in trouble, now you were in

the kitchen trying to find something to eat?" Vonna looked at Pooh then at the social worker but didn't say anything.

"Hey, look at me baby, what happened after that?" Pooh said trying to get her to speak up.

"It's okay baby, don't look at daddy or Ms. Janice, talk to me okay?" Vonna wiped her eyes and nodded.

"I was tryna make a sandwich, but the bread was too far so I got on a box to try to reach it, but I fell, and the hot stuff fell on me." She cried.

"What hot stuff baby?" I asked Vonna.

"The stuff that Nana use when she cooks chicken," Vonna said. This bitch told my daughter to go fix herself something to eat knowing that it was hot fucking grease on the stove. Pooh looked at me with pleading eyes knowing I was about to lose it.

"What happened next?" Pooh said.

"I fell on the floor and cried for my mommy, but she never came, she left with the scary man," at this moment I broke down crying. I couldn't take hearing anymore, I knew that I couldn't hurt Sheila because Vonna still loves her mama, and I couldn't live with myself knowing that I'm the reason why her mama is dead. Vonna noticed me crying and hugged me tight.

"I'm sorry daddy, I didn't mean to make you cry. I won't do it again," I hugged her tight and didn't let her go. This little girl was my fucking world. I would die for her.

"How did you get here Davonna?" Janice asked.

"I walked to the neighbor's house, and she brought me here," My phone started ringing and it was Kj, I hit ignore, but Carter called me as soon as I was about to put my phone in my pocket.

"What?" I said answering my phone.

"The traps was hit and burned down, meet us at the warehouse now nigga," Carter said in one breath. I hung up the phone and sat Vonna down, if it wasn't one thing it was another. I had to worry about Vonna, and my street life, shit was all fucked up now.

"Fuck, aye I gotta go, is that all you needed?" I asked looking at Janice

"Yes, she can leave with you, but I will be in touch to set up a meeting," I was about to grab Vonna but Bianca Pooh stopped me.

"She hasn't been discharged yet," I walked out of the room to find a doctor.

"Excuse me ma'am I'm Davonna's father is she getting discharged this morning?"

"Oh yes sir, it's just going to take a moment for me to get the discharge paper."

"Coo I have to leave, but my friend Bianca is in there have her sign the discharge papers." The doctor nodded then walked away.

"I'm about to go, the doctors will bring you papers to sign to she can be discharged. I'll call my mom to come and get her from my place."

"She can stay with me Dev that's not a problem." Pooh said looking at me while rubbing my back. I grabbed her hand and kissed it, being around her was a great feeling, I couldn't explain it. Every time she touched me my body automatically relaxed.

"Are you sure?" I asked. I didn't want her to feel uncomfortable in my home alone.

"Yes, but we're still going to your place."

"Daddy I don't wanna go back with mommy," Vonna started crying which broke my heart. Pooh unbuckled her seatbelt and turned around to look at Vonna.

"Hey pretty girl, you wanna stay with me at Daddy's house?" Vonna nodded and smiled. Pooh wiped her face and sat back down.

"Daddy huh?" I said smirking at her. She burst out laughing.

"Shut up nigga and get yo ass out!"

. . . .

"Man, what the fuck happened?" I yelled while walking in the warehouse. Everybody had a stale ass expression on their face.

"Man, Rock called while you were at the hospital and said that the traps that Tony was running got hit. When we made it there to check the cameras, they were all turned off," Kj said while rolling up a blunt.

"Hold the fuck on, don't nobody know where the cameras are except for us and most of our trusted men, this shit was an inside job," I said to no one in particular.

"Where the fuck is that nigga Ahmad?" My brother Davon said.

"Nigga what the fuck do you mean where is Ahmad, are you trying to say that our brother had something to do with this shit?" Carter yelled while getting in my brother's face. Me and my brother were the total opposite of each other. Davon reminded me of Kenyon, he was joking all the time even when shit is not funny. That nigga was also reckless as fuck, he would kill you in front of yo kid and not think twice about it.

"My nigga who the fuck is you talking to like that, hell yea I think Ahmad had something to do with it cause his ass ain't here. Carter, you got about thirty seconds to get yo ole Rick James looking ass out my face before Pooh be short a best friend," when He said that we all busted out laughing.

"You can't ever be fucking serious, can you? Carter, you do look like Rick James though," Kenyon said while putting his arm on Carter's shoulder.

"Real shit, I don't think Ahmad would do some shit like that though, I mean I can't stand the nigga, but he loves Pooh too much to do some grimy shit like that, and plus that's our nigga," Kj said while looking at me. Something about that nigga Ahmad is off to me, I can't put my finger on it, but eventually it will come to me. Until then I'm gone stay far away from him.

"What the fuck yall niggas talking about?" I looked towards the door and saw him coming in looking like he hasn't slept.

"Nigga why yo ass coming in here looking like yo stink, and where the fuck have you been?" Kayin ask. Ever since he been here, he hasn't said a word, that's why I could tell that he was mad cause that nigga face turned red a shit.

"Calm yo hostile ass down. I have been looking for Pooh, have yall seen her?" Kenyon and Davon looked at me with smirks on their face. I just shook my head because I know one of them are going to say something ignorant.

"Nah we haven't seen her, Davon have you seen her bro?" Kenyon looked at Davon like he was serious.

"Nah I don't even know her like that, but Killa do. Killa have you seen her bro?" Kenyon burst out laughing like he just heard the best joke.

"Yea I seen her, she should be at the hospital watching Vonna, I'll call her for you," when I said that the two dumb asses busted out laughing. I pulled my phone out of my pocket and dialed B's number. When she answered on the first ring Ahmad looked like he wanted to kill me.

"What's up Dev," unintentionally I smiled as soon as I heard her voice.

"Yo nigga is right here, he said he has been looking for you."

"Tell him I said fuck him, and he better hope I don't tell my brother's about how he been treating me." She yelled then hung up.

"So, do you wanna tell me what she was talking about Ahmad?" Kayin said while getting out of his seat and walking towards Ahmad. He just shook his head and stepped back.

"Nah I'm good. Me and Bianca's business has nothing to do with yall."

"That's where you're wrong, my sister is my business, but I'm not about to stand here and argue with you. I'll just go to my sister and ask her what's going on," when Kj said that I sat down in my chair and smirked. I was about to make Ahmad's day even worse.

"She ain't at home Kj."

"Ahh shit here we go," Kenyon waved his hands in the air and laughed.

"What the fuck you mean she ain't at home, you fucking my wife nigga?" Ahmad got in my face like he was gone do something.

"Kj you better get this nigga out my face before I end his life. Oh, and you don't need to worry about B anymore, she's my girl now bitch," I said to Ahmad then walked off. I'm not about to stand here and argue with another nigga about a woman that's not even his anymore. When I made it to my car, I pulled my phone out of my pocket and saw that Sheila was calling me. I hesitantly answered the phone debating on if I want to kill that bitch.

"What the fuck do you want Sheila?"

"I want my daughter back Killa, when are you bringing her home?"

"Bitch you're not getting her back, you better be lucky I'm not gone kill you, now is that all you want?"

"Can I at least see her Killa, that's still my daughter, I just miss her so much," she tried to cry, but I wasn't falling for it.

"I'll bring her by when I have time but don't call me anymore," I hung up the phone and leaned back on my car. There was a point in time when I could tolerate Sheila, but as time went on, she became harder to deal with.

"Bro are you good?" Davon placed his hand on my shoulder and slightly shook it snapping me out of my thoughts.

"Yea I'm coo what's up though, what are you getting in to tonight?"

"Shit I don't know, probably go to paradise tonight and kick it with Kj." Kj and Carter own one of the biggest clubs in Atlanta called Paradise.

"I might come out tonight, I just need to call ma and see if she can watch Vonna."

"Alright bro just let me know, I'm out of here, Kj probably gone have us up early as fuck in the morning," I nodded my head and got in my car. We need to figure out who we got beef with, because shit is about to get all bad.

CHAPTER 5

Kj

My sister got me fucked up if she thinks I'm about to let whatever this nigga did slide. My sister is my world, and I refused to let anything happen to her. I have three siblings, Kayin, Kenyon, and Pooh. Of course, Pooh's spoiled ass is the youngest of out all of us, our father adopted her when her parents died, she was only twelve years old, and for some reason my mother didn't like her, she treated Pooh like she wasn't shit. It was like she was jealous of the attention that my daddy was giving her. When my dad asked if she could stay with me to avoid fights and argument, of course I said yes, and ever since then she has been more than a sister too me, she was my best friend, rock, lil baby, and my everything. I would go to war for my little sister, so to see that she is letting this nigga treat her like that made me wanna beat her ass. I was sitting in the living room smoking a blunt when Carter walked in and sat next to me.

"What's on yo mind bro? I know you still not tripping on that shit that Pooh said about Ahmad!"

"Man, you not? You know it takes a lot to make her mad, and she didn't even tell us."

"That's not our business Kj, she's grown and y'all need to let her make her own mistakes. Stop treating her like a fucking kid all of the time." I looked at this fool like he was crazy. He is the main one running to her rescue when her ass is being dramatic. Carter was more than my right hand; he was my brother; I trusted this nigga with my life. When my pops took him in after his grandmother died, I knew we were going to be so close. There wasn't a day when Carter was not with me, if you saw me you saw Carter, and if I had beef I promise you that Carter is going to be next to me ready to pull the trigger. That was my nigga and I loved his crazy ass to death.

"Nigga shut yo ass up. If Pooh even get a damn splinter you gone be the first one over there." He just shook his head and laughed because he knows that it's true. When it comes to Pooh can't nobody tell him nothing.

"Nigga fuck you, let's stop talking about her for a moment though. Who do you think is after us?"

"Shit I don't know, but I do agree with Killa and Davon though. It is kind of weird that nobody could get in contact with Ahmad when that was happening, it seems kind of skeptical to me," I don't have nothing against Ahmad, he will always be my nigga, and I appreciate everything that he has done for this family, but today made me look at him different.

"I don't think he's up to no snake shit, he was probably just looking for Pooh, but I'm about to go to bed," he snatched the blunt out of my hand and walked away. I just sat on the couch and chilled until I fell asleep.

• •

The next morning, I woke up to the smell of breakfast, and my mama's loud ass mouth. I got up, walked to the bathroom and handled my hygiene, and walked downstairs to the kitchen when I got done.

"What's up ma dukes," I walked over to the stove and kissed her cheek.

"Hey baby, how have you been?"

"I've been good, but where is my sister at, did she go home?" Pooh came over in the middle of the night crying. I didn't ask her why she was crying I just let her crawl in my bed and cry herself to sleep like she did when we were younger. My mom looked at me like she was confused.

"Baby you don't have a sister," I just looked at her and tried to keep my cool, she knew who I was talking about, and it made me mad that she treats my sister like that for no reason. Pooh has never disrespected her or even gave her a reason to not like her, my mom doesn't even care about that though. Pooh ain't blood so she is not considered family in my mother's eyes.

"I'm talking about Pooh ma," she smacked her lips and continued to cook.

"That fat bitch ain't yo sister, and I sent her ass home," she said nonchalantly.

"Why the fuck...."

"Kj pops want you bro," Carter said as soon as he stepped in the kitchen. He knew I was about to go off that's why he came in here so quickly. I just laughed and walked away.

"What's up old man, lil niggas," I spoke to my pops and brothers.

"Watch that old shit nigga, what's this shit I hear about yall traps getting hit?" I ran my hands down my face and looked my pops right in the eyes.

"I fucked up pops, I let a snake in, and he stole our money, and the product," my pops slammed his fist on the desk and looked at me.

"You damn right you fucked up, what the fuck was you thinking Kj, you know what you weren't fucking thinking!" Getting pissed off and how he was talking to me, I stood up and got in his face. I had respect for my pops, he taught me everything he know, but I'm not about to sit here and let another man disrespect me.

"Yo pops, it's not Kj fault it's me and Kayin's faults, we asked him to put Tony on he tried to...." Kenyon said trying to explain, but my pops cut him off

"Everybody get out except for Kj," Kayin and Kenyon got out, as soon as the door shut my pops threw a pair of gloves at me, and as soon as I put them bitches on, he punched me so hard in the stomach I lost my balance, but I came back in with a mean right hook. Me and pops were going at it until he was tired, I ain't gone lie his old ass got me but his ass was fucked up too.

"Now that you got that out of yo system we can actually talk like real nigga, the reason why I am so hard on you is because you're the oldest and I see a lot of myself in you. I don't want to see you make the same mistake I did when I was your age, I want you to be better than me," Pops said getting all emotional and shit.

"Pops that's the thing I can't be better than you if you keep sheltering me. Every time I fuck up you and my uncles always come and take over, this is my shit, you handed it over to me, let me fix my own fuck up's... Damn pops," He got out of his seat and looked me in my eyes.

"I'm proud of you son, you showed me that you and ready to run this business, and that you are man enough to take care of your responsibilities and fix your mistake. How is my baby girl doing?"

"She's good, spoiled and very crazy, but on some real shit pops, you need to talk to her, she came in my room the other night and cried herself to sleep in my arms because she thinks you don't love her anymore," I told my pops. He thinks that he doesn't need to come around because Pooh is grown now, but that's not the case. Pooh needs her father, there is only so much that I can do when it comes to being there for her. My pops sat back down and ran his hands down his face.

"I never wanted her to think that, I love my daughter with all my heart, I would never stop loving her, I just don't know how to let your mother, or siblings know that she sis my daughter and I love her equally."

"You gone have to talk to ma, she said some shit that got me wanting to stay away from her, she is getting out of hand pops."

"I'll talk to her son," we both got up and walked in the kitchen, as soon as my mom seen my face she flipped out.

"Oh My God what did you do to my baby!" she ran to me and tried to touch my face, but I quickly moved grabbed my keys and left. I love my mama to death, but I will not tolerate her disrespecting Pooh like that, either pops was gone talk to her or I was gone stop fucking with her all together. I texted Carter to see where he was at.

Me: Wya nigga

Carter: Tryna find something to eat. I had to leave ma was on some other shit

Me: Already know, meet me at Pooh's house, Let Killa, and Davon know.

Carter: Bet

As soon as I pulled up at Pooh's house and smelled the food from outside, I quickly used my key to unlock the door and walked straight to the kitchen. Pooh was at the stove cooking some fried potatoes, she looked over her shoulder smiled and continued to cook, I just smiled and watched her cook. I already know that the things that my mama said got to her, but she just learns to brush it off.

"I'm sorry about my mom's sis," she looked at me and came to sit on my lap.

"It's okay brother, I don't trip on that anymore, that's why I came home and cooked, I knew you was coming over," she kissed my cheek and smiled.

"Where yo pussy ass man at?" I asked referring to Ahmad. She looked at me and rolled her eyes.

"That's not my man anymore and he haven't been here."

"When I see him, I'm gone beat his ass," she rolled her eyes and looked away.

"Let me go fix our plate before Carter's hungry ass come over here and eat everything up," she got up and fixed both of our plates. I was about to go in the living room and watch tv, but

I heard Carter's loud ass voice come through the front door.

"I know you ain't in here cooking and didn't fix me shit," Carter said while walking in right along with Ashton.

"What's up big head, hey best friend," Ashton came over kissed my cheek and smacked pooh on the ass.

"Hey everyone," I turned around and saw the most beautiful women I have ever seen, Shorty was dark chocolate, short, thick in all the right places, big brown eyes, and a smile to die for. I was staring so hard Carter stood in front of me and laughed.

"Damn Kj close your mouth before something fly in it," Carter said with a smirk on his face. I pushed him out the way and focused on her sexy ass again

"Yo shorty what's your name?" She looked at me and rolled her eyes.

"Not interested" She put her hand in my and was about to walk away, but Pooh stopped her.

"Bitch I will drop you where you stand if you ever put yo hand in my brother's face again," I got up and pushed Pooh behind me cause her crazy ass was about to beat this bitch's ass.

"Calmed down Pooh, she is not worth it."

"Who is this bitch anyways?" Pooh asked while snatching away from me. Carter got up and walked towards this girl.

"Pooh this is my best friend Staci, Staci this is...."

"Best friend?" Pooh said looking between her and Carter confused. I calmly got up and stood to the side.

"Ah shit Ashton get over here and get out the way cause shit was about to hit the fan." I saw the Kayin and Kenyon come in, so I told them to come in and shut up.

"Did you say best friend?" Pooh tilted her head to the side waiting on him so respond.

"Yes, that's what I said, what's wrong with me having two best friends Pooh?" Carter dumb ass said. Pooh didn't say anything, she nodded her head, got up and walked out.

"Nigga are you stupid?" I asked while staring at him.

"What did I do? Pooh know we have only been best friends for 4 years but me and Staci been best friends since kids. Staci and I got that connection that me and Pooh don't have. I love Staci to death, I know she would go to war for me, but I don't know if Pooh would do the same," I just looked at him like he lost his mind.

"Wow, is that really what you think of me Carter, you know what, I'm not going to waste my energy on responding." I looked at my sister and she had tears streaming down her face. That shit made me mad as fuck.

"Are you okay sis?" I asked but she was too busy looking at Carter then Ashton. She walked over to Ash and slapped her ass so hard that she had my fucking hand hurting

"Bitch you knew?"

"I promise I didn't Pooh," Ash said while crying.

"Yall are so fucking dramatic, damn yall act like yall fucking or something," Kenyon's ignorant ass said while fixing his plate, but he was telling the truth. I feel so bad for my sister. Her and Carter were so close you would think they were dating, but that's not the case. As soon as I was about to kick Carter's ass my ex texted me

Alicia: Hey, we need to talk ASAP

Me: About what Licia?

Alicia was my first love, we been through hell and back with each other, she just couldn't be with me because I was in the streets, and I was not about to change my life because she wasn't happy with what I did.

Alicia: It's about Pooh, please come over Kj

Me: I'm on my way

I wonder what the problem could be, her and Pooh don't even like each other.

CHAPTER 6

Pooh

"**B**abe are you okay?" Ash said while walking in my room. I wanted to tell her I was but honestly, I wasn't. That shit that Carter said really hurt me, I just can't believe that he said some of the things that came out of his mouth. I love Carter, but I think I need to stay away from him for a while.

"I'll be okay my love, what are you doing today?" She took her shoes off and climbed in my bed. I scooted close to her and laid my head on her shoulder.

"I was gone chill with Carter but since he pissed my sister off, I'm not fucking with him." I shot my head up so fast I thought I was gone break my neck. Did she say she was gone "*chill*" with carter?

"Bitch what do you mean you was gone chill with Carter, yall not that close."

"Um me and Carter have been kicking it, we wanted to tell you, but I told him to wait."

"What do you mean wait Ash, do you know how long I have been waiting for yall to get together?" Ever since Carter met Ash, he has been trying to get her, but her stubborn ass was not having it, she said that he was crazy, which I thought was funny cause she is crazy too. Every time they were around each other they always argued and flirted with each other. That's why I'm trying to figure out what took them so long.

"I really like him Pooh, and I just didn't wanna jinx it you know. Even though he is crazy and has a couple of screws loose, he knows how to treat me, he is a gentleman, and he treats me with so much respect it's crazy. I want to give him all of me, but I'm scared to."

"Ash, Carter is my best friend and I know him better then he knows himself. When he loves he loves hard, he will never hurt you intentionally, but if you keep your guard up eventually, he will leave you alone. I may not like his trifling ass right now, but I know that he is a good man. Give him a chance, he has been chasing after you for like what five years now? Give him a chance baby." She was about to respond but my bedroom door flew open and Ahmad was standing there looking like he wanted to murder me.

"Ashton will you please give me and Bianca some time alone?" When I looked at Ahmad, I seen nothing but darkness in his eyes. I put my hand over my growing belly and prayed that Ahmad didn't put his hands on me. Ash looked at me with questioning eyes.

"GET THE FUCK OUT NOW ASHTON!" He pulled his gun out and aimed it at her head. Her crazy ass just laughed and walked out slowly making sure she bumps into him in the process. When she closed the door, he leaned on the dresser and looked at me.

"Where have you been Bianca? I have been looking for you."

"Not here, why are you worried about it Ahmad? You haven't been home either, and you look like you stink. You been at that bitch Heather's house huh, three years, THREE FUCK-ING YEARS AHMAD! Three years that I waisted being faithful to you, I gave you everything, every fucking thing that I had, I lost count of how many times I fell out with my brothers because of yo stupid ass, but for what, to get cheated on? I have been nothing but faithful to you, when we lost Makenzie, I wanted to give up on having children, but I didn't because YOU wanted more kids. I cook, clean, wash yo clothes, fuck and suck you whenever you want me to, but what do I get in return? A broken heart, I gave you everything, I trusted you." I broke down crying. I didn't realize that I could hurt this much, I loved him with everything in me, I gave this man my life, my world, my heart, and he played with it like it was a toy. He walked over to me and tried to touch me, but I quickly snatched away.

"Baby let me explain please, she doesn't mean anything to me I promise. You are my world I would die for you and my seeds; I didn't mean anything that I told her. Stop crying baby you know I hate when you cry, come here." He grabbed me and pulled me in to his chest. I tried to fight him off, but I couldn't I was too weak. Ahmad was my world, and I couldn't see life without him in it.

"Ahmad stop please, let me go! I hate you so much, why did you do this to me?" I cried hard. I fell on the floor and just laid there and cried.

"Baby please get up I'm sorry." He picked me up and laid me in the bed, he stripped out of his clothes, laid his phone on the dresser and got in bed with me. I just laid my head on his chest and cried. I can't believe that he actually cheated on me. The more I thought about it, the more pissed I got. After a while that hurt turned in to anger and I wanted to kill his ass. I laid there for an hour until I knew he was sleep. I slowly got up making sure not to wake him and walked to the kitchen. I went to the cabinet pulled out a pot and filled it with hot water. I put it on the stove and waited until the water started boiling, once it was hot enough for me, I carried the water upstairs and just stood over Ahmad's cheating ass. I sat the water down and pulled the covers back. I picked the pot up and dumped it on his naked body. As soon as the water touched his skin, he let out a high pitch scream and jumped up so fast.

"Ahhhh shit! Bitch what the fuck is wrong with you?" He ran towards the bathroom and turned on the cold water. I doubled over in laughter which pissed him off even more.

"That's what yo cheating ass get nigga! You thought I was

gone let you off the hook like that? You better be lucky that's all I did, I'm so fucking done with you Ahmad, ugh three fucking years." He got out the shower and ran towards me. When he made it to me, he wrapped his hands around my neck and squeeze tightly. I tried to pry his hands from around my neck, but it was too late, Ahmad was gone, I was looking in the eyes of the devil, and I knew it was gone take a miracle for Ahmad to come back to his senses.

"If you weren't pregnant with my babies, I would kill you, now when I let you go you better not hit me do you understand me?" I nodded my head and tried not to cry. When he let me go, I fell to the floor, and gasped for air.

"You better be lucky I didn't kill yo dumb ass for doing that shit, get yo ass up and change the sheets." He walked in the bathroom and locked the door. I walked over to the dresser and looked me myself in the mirror, I had a bruise on my neck so big that you could see his handprints. I shook my head and walked out of the room to get another set of sheets. I walked back to my room and seen his phone ringing. I tried to ignore it, but I couldn't help myself. I quickly picked it up and answered without looking at the screen.

"Hello?" I answered trying to fight back the tears.

"What the fuck is wrong with you Bianca!" I looked at the phone and saw that it was Kayin.

"Nothing, what's up?"

"Don't fucking play with me, what did that nigga do?" I could tell in my brother's voice that he knew something was wrong, so I had to think of something.

"He didn't do anything Kayin I'm just in a little pain."

"Mmhmm you better not be fucking lying, where is he at?"

"In the shower, hold on." I walked to the bathroom and knocked on the door.

"What!"

"Kayin is on the phone!" He opened the door and grabbed the phone. He was standing there butt ass naked with his third leg standing at attention. Even though I wanted to kill him right now, the thought of him being deep inside of me had me instantly wet. He looked down and smirked.

"Nah yo ass ain't getting none." He smirked then slammed the door in my face. Hurt couldn't even explain the way I was feeling right now. I walked back over to the bed, changed the sheets grabbed my phone, and went downstairs in his man cave. Once I had the tv on I got comfortable in his chair, I picked my phone up and dialed Devin's number.

"What's up B, are you okay?" He started asking as soon as he answered the phone.

"Yes, I'm okay, I was actually calling to talk to Vonna."

"Oh, I'm not at home, I'm with yo brother's but when I get home, I'll have her call you."

"Okay that's all I wanted."

"Damn mama you don't want to talk to me, you only using me for my daughter? That's fucked up." He said sounding like his feelings were hurt.

"Nigga I know yo ass ain't over there crying because she doesn't wanna talk to you! Damn sis what the fuck are you doing to these gay ass niggas," I busted out laughing at Kenyon's crazy ass.

"Something is wrong with my brother, of course I want to talk to you, but I know you're busy soo." I looked at the door and seen Ahmad standing at the bottom of the chairs.

"Umm I got to go," Not giving him a chance to respond I quickly hung up and looked at Ahmad, but he just laughed and walked over to me.

"Damn so you gone talk to another nigga in our house?"

"Ahmad please don't," I begged already knowing that I was about to get my ass beat.

"Bitch shut yo hoe ass up, you don't wanna be with me anymore Bianca?" I shook my head no with caused him to chuckle. I was about to get up, but the next thing I felt was his fist connecting with my jaw. Screaming in pain I tried to get up but there was no use, I just laid on the floor protecting my stomach. Eventually he stopped, and just stood over me.

"If you even think about leaving me, I will fucking kill you, do you understand me." He asked calmly. I just laid there without answering his question.

"Bitch I guess you couldn't hear me so let me just say it again! I WILL KILL YOU IF YOU EVEN THINK ABOUT LEAVING ME! Now do you understand?" He grabbed me by my hair and forced me to look at him.

"Yes, I hear you."

"Good, now I'm about to go with yo bitch ass brothers, I'll be back" he kissed my forehead and walked out the room. Waiting until I heard the front door closed, I got up and tried to reach for my phone, but I felt myself slipping away. As soon as I pick up my phone, I quickly tried to dial my daddy's number.

"What's up Mama, I should beat yo ass for hanging up on me." Realizing I dialed Devin's number I tried to hang up but couldn't my eyes were swollen shut and I couldn't see.

"Bianca, Bianca are you okay?"

"El hel"

"What, talk to me mama?"

"Help me!" I barely got out before everything went black.

CHAPTER 7

Killa

"**W**hat the fuck was that Killa?" Kj shouted from across the table.

"Bro I don't know, it sounded like she was saying help me." I said in a panic tone. Kayin got up and punched a hole in the wall.

"If this nigga put his hands on my sister, I'm gone kill his ass." We all got up and headed towards the door. When we made it outside Ahmad was pulling up with a frown on his face.

"Where the fuck yall nigga's going?" Kenyon rushed over towards him and started beating his ass.We stood there for a minute until Carter and Kayin pulled him up. Kj, Davon, and I just stood around and watched.

"Nigga what the fuck happened to my best friend, you know what you been on some Snake shit lately, what the fuck is going on with you?" Carter asked with his gun aimed at Ahmad's head. Ahmad just stood up and laughed while spitting the blood out of his mouth.

"You gone shoot me Carter, over some bitch? You know what fuck all yall niggas, you better be lucky all I did was beat her ass and not kill her for talking back to me, well she may not be alive," When he said that I blacked out and started beating his ass, I don't remember shit but Davon and Kj pushing me inside of my car. I was trying so hard to get out, but Davon wouldn't let me go.

"Davon get the fuck off me bro."

"Nah I'm good, you need to calm yo ass down, so we can go to the hospital, and you got to explain to Pooh why her nigga is practically dead."

"That nigga needs a life alert button," I couldn't help but laugh at Kenyon.

"Nigga shut yo ass up and come on before I beat yo ass too," everybody got in the car and drove to the hospital. When we pulled up to the hospital Kj and Carter were the first people out of the car.

"Nigga you getting out?" Kayin ask while rolling up a blunt. Honestly, I didn't know if I wanted to get out and see B like that, I'm really feeling her, and that shit is fucking with me.

"Yea man I just need some time, I don't think I wanna see her like that."

"You feeling my sister huh?" I chuckled and ran my hands down my face.

"Yea man I'm feeling her, but she needs to get over that pussy boy before we even think about getting to know each other more."

"Shit I understand, and plus I don't think she wants him now. Speaking of Ahmad, I got a feeling we gone have to kill his ass pretty soon."

"Man, what is going on with that nigga? I never liked his ass, but he never seemed like a snake until now," before my family moved out here, I heard of Ahmad, and from my knowledge he was like family and shit. So, for him to be acting shady to the people who has been feeding him is kind of fuck up.

"I feel the same way bro, the only difference is me and my brothers grew up with Ahmad. His ass is like our brother, so I don't know what has got into him, but I'm going to find out. Come on let's go in here before Kj bring his ass out here," we both got out the car and made our wait in the hospital, when we reached the waiting room everyone was in there except for her daddy and Kj.

"Where pops and Kj?" Kayin asked.

"In the room with Pooh," Kenyon answered.

"How is she, how are my nephews doing?" Kenyon put his head down and shook his head.

"She's in room two-thirteen bro," he said looking between me and Kayin. When I made it to the room I just stood there contemplating on what to do next, and as soon as I was about to turn around my uncle came out the room.

"Nephew where you going?"

"Man, Unc I can't see her like that, just tell her I came by."

"You don't think it was hard to see my daughter like that? You gone have to suck that shit up and go in there, she needs everybody's support right now," I nodded my head and walked through the door. When I seen her face, I wanted to go and find that nigga Ahmad and kill his ass myself.

"Don't look at me like I'm ugly nigga," B said while trying to smile.

"Shut yo goofy ass up, how are you feeling."

"Like I just got my ass beat, where is Kayin at?"

"I'm the waiting room, how are the babies, what happened?"

"They are okay surprisingly, and I don't wanna talk about that right now, I appreciate you coming to see me though," I walked over to her and kissed her forehead. I sat in the chair besides her bed and held her hand, I felt like she was trying to get rid of me, but it was not going to be that easy, so I just sat down and held her hand.

"You already know I was coming up here, you know I'm gone have to kill his ass, right?"

"I honestly don't care anymore, I'm tired of saving him, but I do want you and my brothers to stay away from him, he's not right in the head."

"Oh, I think we found that out today, but don't worry

about that, you just need to focus on you and those lil niggas right now."

"I know, Kj is making me move back in with him unfortunately. I don't want to, but I don't really have a choice," she rolled her eyes and put her hand over her fat belly.

"When are they letting you go?"

"They want to keep me over night for some observations, hopefully they discharge me in the morning."

"I would stay with you, but I have to get Vonna, do you need anything?"

"Some Chinese food sound good right now!" She closed her eyes and licked her lips.

"Alright crazy girl, I'll bring you some back." I kissed her forehead and walked out the room. Seeing B like that really did something to me, I felt like I wasn't there to protect her, I mean I barley know this girl, but I feel like I have to do everything in my power to protect her. I haven't felt like this about a female in a long time, and it really do scare me, the last time I had feelings for somebody was when I fell in love with the city hoe. I told myself that I would never be in a relationship with anybody else but look at me now.

"Yo I have to go get Vonna, what are y'all getting in to tonight?" I said while walking in the waiting room.

"Shit we might just chill up here with Pooh, I don't think we are in the mood to kick it tonight." Carter said speaking for everybody. Carter never was the talkative type growing up, he would always stay in the background and just chill. Don't get me wrong this nigga is crazy as fuck, but he was never the social type, every time they came to visit my family he would always stay to his self, that's what I liked about him.

"Alright coo, I'll probably bring Vonna back up here then." I walked out the hospital and got in my car. Once I was settled, I pulled out my phone and called my mama.

"Hey son"

"Hey ma I'm on my way to get Vonna."

"Okay baby, how is Pooh doing?"

"She's okay the babies are fine, they are just keeping her overnight for some observations."

"Well that's good, alright boy I'll see you when you get here."
. . . .

"Ma where you at!" The smell of soul food invaded my nose which caused my stomach to grumble.

"I'm in the kitchen Devin and stop yelling before you wake my grandchild up," I walked in the kitchen and saw my mama standing over the stove cooking.

"What you in here cooking," I kissed her cheek then sat down on the bar stool.

"Roast, potatoes, fried chicken, cabbage, and corn bread, want some?"

"You know I want some, make B a plate too." My mama looked at me over her shoulder and smiled. My mama's smile will light up the whole room.

"What are you smiling at old lady."

"You like Pooh, don't you?" I was debating on talking to my mama about this, because she can be dramatic at times.

"Honestly, I do ma, I don't know what to do though, she just got out of a relationship with that nigga Ahmad, and plus she's pregnant with his kids. She is going through a lot right now and I don't know what to do." I'm usually the type of nigga to go after what I want but it's different this time. I want B so bad, but honestly, I'm scared that one of us is gone get hurt in the end. There are four things I don't play about, my family, money, daughter, and my trust. If you fuck with any of those things, I will kill you with no hesitation. If I do decide to give me and B a chance, I know I'm about to be risking a lot of shit. I just don't know what to do right now.

"Well I can tell you that Pooh is a very sweet and honest girl. She wouldn't do anything to hurt you intentionally, and If you really wanna be with her you must be willing to give her a chance and understand that she is not perfect. You also have to understand that she is going to have ties with Ahmad for eighteen years, is that something you can deal with?" Ahmad's snake ass might not even live to see his kids being born so I'm not worried about that. We will just have to cross that bridge when we get there.

"I don't know ma, I'm not talking about marrying the girl, I just want to get to know her more and see where this takes us. You and pops know her better than I do, yall need to be the ones telling me if it's a good idea." She handed me my plates and laughed.

"Boy you are grown; your father and I cannot tell you who you can and can't date. Shit we tried to tell you not to mess with Sheila, but you didn't listen. Speaking of Sheila have you talked to her?"

"Nah I haven't, and I don't plan to any time soon." Sheila has been blowing up my phone since I took my daughter, and I'll be damn if I let her go back. I might let her come see Vonna, but right now I'm not ready for that, I might kill the bitch.

"Now Devin I know she was wrong for what she did, but you must understand that Davonna is her child to, and you just can't take her away because she made a one little mistake." I just grabbed my plate and got up, not wanting to hear anything else I walked away and went to find Vonna. I saw her sleep on the couch cuddled up with my pops.

"Vonna wake baby girl," I kissed her cheek, which caused her to open her eyes and smile.

"Hi daddy!" Her goofy self-giggled and kissed my cheek.

"What's up princess, you ready to go?"

"Yes sir, are we going to see Pooh!"

"Yes, but we are going to go see Mommy first," she looked at me like she wanted to say no, but she just nodded her head instead.

"Daddy's not leaving you over there baby, mommy just miss you."

"You promise."

"I promise baby girl now come on," I put her down and helped her out the door and inside the car. Once she was in her seat I got in the car and drove off. By the time we made it to Sheila house Vonna was already sleep. I hate that Sheila had to move down here with me but that was the only way I would be in my child's life. Now I'm stuck with her nasty hoe ass, I walked up to the door and used my key to get in.

"Sheila where you at?"

"Here I come daddy," I just shook my head and sat down at the table. As soon as Sheila seen me, she tried to reach for Vonna, but I slapped her hand.

"Come on Killa don't do that to me, let me hold her please."

"Nah I'm good you can see her from right here," Sheila smacked her lips and snatched Vonna out my hand.

"Nigga you can't tell me shit about my daughter, wake up Vonna Pooh." She tickled Vanna's stomach which caused her beautiful brown eyes to open. As soon as she made eye contact with Sheila she tried to wiggle out of her embrace, but Sheila wasn't having it.

"Sheila give her here. She doesn't want you and if you make her cry, I'm gone beat yo ass."

"Can Mommy have a hug?" Vonna looked at me with questionable eyes. I nodded my head, so she can hug her back.

"I missed you so much, go play in your room while I talk

to daddy okay." She nodded her head and walked over to me.

"Promise you won't leave me daddy?"

"I promise baby girl."

"We going to see Pooh later?" Her eyes lit up just by talking about her which made me smile.

"Yes baby now go play," I kissed her cheek and she took off running. When she was gone, I looked at Sheila, and she looked like she wanted to murder me.

"I don't want that bitch around my child Devin."

"Bitch who are you to tell me who I can and can't have my daughter around? She doesn't even wanna stay with you, so what makes you think you got some say so in her life?"

"IM HER MOTHER KILLA!" She got up and screamed.

"Were you her mother when she got burned with hot grease, exactly so get the fuck out my face with all that bullshit Sheila, you better be lucky I'm letting you see her now."

"That was an accident Killa, when are you gone let that go, mothers fuck up." I was about to respond but I felt my phone vibrating in my pocket. I pulled my phone out and smile at the name.

"What's up mama?"

"Where is my food at?" Hearing her angelic voice come through my phone silent chills down my body.

"Chill out lil nigga, I had to go get Vonna from my mama house."

"Did she cook?"

"Yea and I got you a plate."

"Yasssss! Yo mama cooking is fire! Alright hurry up so I can eat and love on my baby some." Hearing her refer to Vonna as her baby made me blush. "Alright we on our way." I hung up the phone and smiled.

"Nigga you got me fucked up if you think I'm about to let you take my baby to go see her," Sheila yelled while getting in my face.

"Sheila move before I beat yo ass, Vonna come on, it's time to go!"

"You ain't taking my baby around her, I'm calling the Police." As soon as she said that I knew she wanted to take it back. I smirked at walked closer to her.

"You better watch what you say because it ain't shit for me to snap yo neck right now. Vonna don't fuck with you anymore and she is the reason why you are alive, now what was that you said?" She shook her head and cried.

"I didn't say anything."

"Good girl, now don't give me a reason to have to kill you okay."

"I'm ready daddy!" I looked down at Vonna and smiled. I kissed Sheila's cheek and walked out the door with my daughter. Once I was in the car, I grabbed my phone and dialed Kj's number.

"What's up?"

"Have somebody watch Sheila, I think her ass is up to something."

"What do you mean bro, you think she is being sneaky?"

"Shit probably, she said something about the feds."

"Say no more, I'll have Rock go over there."

"Good looking out," I hung up the phone and drove off. I couldn't wait to get to the hospital to see my future wife.

CHAPTER 8

Sheila

"This nigga got me fucked up if he thinks I'm about to sit here and watch this bitch play mama to my fucking daughter." I paced back and forth contemplating on what I should do next. I thought about going to the police, but I know Killa would kill me with no hesitation.

"I'm still not understanding why you are so mad about Killa not letting you see Vonna," My boyfriend Richard said.

"I'm not mad about that Richard, I'm mad that he got that bitch playing mama to my child," he looked at me without saying anything, then burst out laughing.

"You dead ass serious right now, Sheila, you don't even want her so why are you worried about who he got around her, you still wanna be with this nigga?"

"Of course, not baby, you know you're the only one for me," truth be told I did wanna be with Killa, but the only thing that's stopping me from being with him is our daughter Davonna. Don't get me wrong, I love my daughter I just don't like her cock blocking ass. Every time I try to get at Killa here she comes always asking for shit, and just like a damn dog he follows up behind her.

"Yea alright, tell that lie to somebody else, you ain't stupid though, you know I would kill you and that nigg,." I put my hand over my mouth trying not to laugh, this pussy ass nigga wouldn't even hurt a fly.

"Richard baby I love you, but you know you're not going to do anything."

"Exactly, so you can sit to ass down and let me handle this," Ahmad said while walking in the door.

"Ahmad how the fuck did you get in my house and what are you doing here?" I asked confused.

"Killa had somebody watching your house so I told them to leave cause I'm watching you, but that's not why I'm here. The reason why I'm here is because I want yall to team up with me to take those niggas down."

"Wait I thought those were your brothers, why are you doing that to them?" He chuckled then pulled a blunt out of his pocket.

"Them niggas were my brothers, but they fucked up when they turned their backs on me as soon as Killa and Davon moved here, and made my bitch break up with me. I want to take them out and get what is owed to me."

"And what is that?" Richard asked interested.

"The family business, so are yall in or out?"

"Shit I'm in, I don't fuck with those niggas anyway." They both looked at me waiting on me to respond. I honestly didn't know what I wanted, a part of me wanted to help kill them, but I couldn't see my life without Killa even though he treats me like shit.

"Give me a minute to think this over."

"What the fuck do you have to think about Sheila?" Richard yelled while getting in my face.

"You're not understanding what I'm saying, Killa is the father of my child and how am I supposed to tell her that I killed her father, let me sleep on it okay?" I wrapped my arms around his neck and pecked his lips.

"Yea whatever Sheila," he said then walked away with Ahmad, I sat on the couch contemplating on my neck move.

CHAPTER 9

Kj

4 months later

"Will you hurry yo ass up!" I yelled as Pooh struggled to walk up the stairs to Carter's home.

"Shut up Ka'Mari, I'm not in the mood for yo shit today, I'm tired, hot, and hungry!" I just shook my head and waited for her to come to the door. She is currently nine months pregnant, so she is doing everything slower than usual.

"Damn yo ass took too long," I said playfully. She mushed me in my head and forced her way inside, before plopping down on the couch and laid her head on Carter's shoulder.

"What yall niggas doing here?" Carter asked while putting the blunt out that he was smoking on.

"We got bored, and she was getting on my nerves," Pooh flipped me off and got up to go in the kitchen.

"So, what's up bro, what's been going on?" Carter said.

"Nothing much just chilling, have you heard from that nigga Ahmad?"

"Nah I haven't heard from that fool since he beat Pooh's ass. I've been trying to talk to him, but he claims he has been busy." That shit that happened four months ago left a bad taste in my mouth. Ahmad was up to some sneaky shit, and brother or not, I don't mind putting a bullet in his head.

"Some shit ain't adding up with him, Ima have Rock stop by his house today," I said while pulling my phone out and shooting Rock a text. There was a knock at the door, and we were too lazy to get up, so we just let the person knock.

"Oh, don't get up yall, I'll get it," Pooh sarcastically said while answering the door. It was that girl Staci looking sexy as fuck.

"May I help you sir?" Pooh's petty as said.

"Um I was actually here to see Carter," Pooh looked back at Carter then walked away.

"What's going on Stac?"

"Well I was actually coming to chill, but I don't feel like arguing with yo best friend."

"No, it's okay, you can stay, her fat ass is too tired to argue." I said while grabbing her hand and pulling her in the house. I looked at Carter with a get the fuck outlook.

"Come on Pooh let's go in the theater and watch a movie," Carter said while getting up.

"Okay bestfriend grab my food and come on." Pooh got up and mushed me before walking away. I sat next to Staci and looked at her.

"Will you stop staring at me like that?" Staci said while shifting in her seat.

"My bad ma, I've just never seen anybody as beautiful as you," she looked at me, then busted out laughing.

"Nigga please try that shit with a dumb bitch, cause I'm not falling for it."

"What do you mean shorty, I'm being serious as fuck." She rolled her eyes and scooted away from me.

"Damn shorty it's like that?"

"Sure is, but what's up, why did you tell me to stay if you were gone be a creep?"

"I wanted to get to know you better, can I take you out some time?" She looked like she was thinking about it which was a good sign.

"I mean I guess you can, but it has to be somewhere public."

"What do you mean somewhere public, you don't want to be alone with me?"

"Nigga I don't know you like that, you're probably crazy and like to sniff bitch's panties." When she said that I busted out laughing.

"Yo you're crazy for real, here put yo number in my phone and I'll call you," She put her number in my phone and we continued to talk until it was time for her to go.
. . . .
"What the fuck are yall dusty ass niggas doing?" Kenyon said while walking in, behind him was Kayin, Killa, Davon, and Ash.

"Hey Kj, where is Pooh at?" Ash said while walking over to me and kissing me on my cheek.

"She is upstairs sleep, don't go up there messing with her Ash, she's been acting crazy since we got here," of course, Ash ignored me and walked upstairs.

"So what's going on Kj, why did you call us here?" Kayin's inpatient ass asked. Sometimes I had to remember that I was the oldest, he thinks just because I'm calmer than him, he can boss me around, but that was not going to work with me so of course I had to check him.

"I don't know who the fuck you think you're talking to, but you need to fix yo tone lil nigga!"

"Fuck you Kj, you called us over here for a reason, and when I asked you what's going on you get a fucking attitude, I got shit to do," tired of hearing his smart ass mouth I walked towards him and pulled him out of his seat.

"You don't have shit to do but sit here and listen to me until I tell you to leave. You don't run shit but yo mouth Kayin, now sit yo ass down and I dare you to try me," Kayin mugged me before pushing me out his face while sitting down. Don't get me wrong, Kayin don't back down from anybody, but he knows if he tries anything with me, I will kick his ass.

"Nigga you're a fucking pussy, how are you gone let Kj punk you Debo?" Kenyon said while laughing. I just shook my head and started the conversation.

"So, the reason why I called yall here is because I need to talk to yall about what's been on my mind."

"What's good bro, are you good?" Kayin asked totally forgetting about his attitude that he previously had. That's one thing that I love about my family, we set aside our differences and come together to defeat our enemies.

"Yea bro I'm good, I just wanted to put a bug in yall ear. Yall know we haven't seen Ahmad in four months, right?" Just like I suspected they all just looked at me waiting for me to finish talking.

"Like I was saying I think he is up to something cause that nigga has been to quiet, and we all know how that nigga gets."

"Man, that's the same thing I said, it's not like Ahmad to stay low for this long, that nigga got something up his sleeve," Kenyon said.

"Especially since this bullshit started with Pooh, you know he is crazy about that girl, he would turn on anybody when it comes to her," Kayin said while rolling up a blunt.

"What are yall niggas talking about?" Pooh said while walking over to Killa and sitting on his lap. Ever since they met, they have been inseparable, and my sister seems happy. They claim that they are not together, but the way they act with each other sounds differently.

"Ahmad," I said while looking at her in the eyes to see how she would react. Even though she claims that she is over Ahmad, we all know that she was crazy over him, and he was her weakness.

"What about him?" She asked trying to sound un-interested.

"Well I was saying that he must be up to something be-cause we haven't heard from him in four months," I said.

"He just called me this morning checking on me." She said nonchalantly.

"Why didn't you say shit?" Killa asked sounding irritated.

"Excuse me, I didn't know I had to check in with yall when I talk to my baby daddy."

"Well you do know Pooh, you're so naive it's embarrass-ing, do you realize that the only reason why he is still contact-ing you is to see what we are up too? His ass is not loyal to us anymore," Kayin all but yelled.

"Whatever yall got going on has nothing to do with our relationship," as soon as the word relationship came out of her mouth she automatically stopped talking and looked at Killa.

"Damn so you're still in a relationship with that nigga after he beat yo ass, you sound dumb as fuck right now." Killa said while shaking his head.

"No Dev that's not what I meant at all," she said sounding like she is trying to convince herself more than anybody else.

"But it's what you said, watch out dude, I don't even wanna be around you right now." He nudged her enough to make her get up, she walked up the stairs with her head held down. My phone vibrated notifying me that I had a message.

Pops: MEET ME AT MY HOUSE RIGHT NOW!

"Am I the only one who just got that message?' I asked looking around at everyone who had their phones in their hands.

"Nah I think we all got it," Kayin said while getting up. Whatever my pops need to talk to us about I'm pretty sure it's not good.

CHAPTER 10

Pooh

"**A**sh I just fucked up big time," laying on Ash's shoulder, I closed my eyes trying to fight back the tears that were threating to fall. I honestly didn't mean to make Devin upset by saying that I was in a relationship with Ahmad, that was a bad habit that I need to break.

"When was the last time you talked to Ahmad before this morning?"

"Two months ago, Ash I really didn't mean to say that I was in a relationship with him," I cried harder. Ash laid her head on my head and just let me cry. The door flew open and Dev was standing there looking like he wanted to murder me.

"We are about to go to yo pops house, are you going or am I dropping you off at the house?"

"You can drop me off at the house, I don't wanna be bothered with people right now," he nodded and turned around to leave.

"Bitch yo better suck the shit out of his dick in the car, because that nigga looks like he wanna beat yo ass. I'm glad Carter and I don't have those type of problems, my ass would've had lock jaw if that was the case," Ash said while getting up and taking her closed off. I just shook my head and left the room. Once I made it out the door and outside, I saw that Dev already had my car door open. He was leaning on it while talking to Davon, I walked over to him and wrapped my arms around his waist. He looked at me then continued to talk to his brother, I just sighed and got in the car. I can't stand when he is mad at me, it drives me insane. Seconds later Dev got in the car and drove off.

"Baby I really didn't mean anything by it I promise, I only want you," he didn't respond, he just continued to drive while bobbing his head to the music.

"Baby can you please talk to me?" I begged once again he ignored me and turned the music up. I laid my head on the seat, looked out the window, and let the tears flow from out of my eyes until I eventually fell asleep in the car.

"Best friend wake yo fat ass up!" Hearing Carter's annoying ass voice made me instantly wake up. Looking around confused, I noticed that I was still in the car in front of my daddy's house.

"What do you want Carter?"

"Killa has been here for thirty minutes now, why the fuck are you still in the car?"

"I fell asleep and his ignorant ass didn't wake me up," I got out the car and followed Carter into the house. The smell of my daddy's spaghetti invaded my nostrils and made my stomach growl and caused my mouth to water. Once I made my way towards the kitchen I stopped when I saw his wife standing at the stove.

"What are you doing in my house Bianca, didn't I tell you that you were not invited over here?" His mama fussed. Laughing sarcastically my petty ass knocked over the plate off the table that I'm guessing was hers. I sat in the chairs and kicked over the one that was next to me.

"Lil mama this is not your house, this is my daddy's house and I can be anywhere I want to be in this mother fucka," I seriously cannot stand this bitch; she makes my skin crawl.

"You really do have a smart-ass mouth, and if I were you, I would be quiet before you write a check that yo ass can't cash."

"Bitch bring it with yo old ass, just because I'm pregnant and yo ass is pushing ninety don't mean I won't kick yo ass," I yelled while getting out my chair. I'm tired of her thinking she can talk to me crazy just because I'm trying to respect my daddy and brothers wishes and not kill her.

"What the fuck is going on in here!" My daddy yelled while walking in the kitchen. Everybody else walked in behind him shaking their heads.

"I'm tired of YOUR daughter disrespecting me like I want kick her ass Ka'Mari!" She yelled which caused me to laugh at her. I walked over to the stove to fix me a plate completely unfazed.

"Pooh did you throw this plate and chair on the floor?" He asked with his arms folded.

"No sir, I did not," I smirked.

"BIANCA!"

"What daddy? I didn't throw it on the floor, I knock them down," I said seriously. Kenyon and Davon's Silly ass burst out laughing which caused me to laugh.

"Really Kenyon, this shit is not funny at all," my daddy fussed while cleaning the mess that I mad.

"My bad pops, but yo daughter is crazy, who the fucks do this kind of petty shit?" He shook his head and went to fix his plate.

"I'm sorry daddy, but your wife needs to know how to re-spect people, I wouldn't have to act like this every time I come over here if she would just stay in her room," I rolled my eyes and sat down to eat. As soon as I was about to put the spaghetti in my mouth my fucking water broke.

"Shit, I didn't even get to eat my damn food, come on and take me to the hospital before I have these babies on yo floor daddy," everybody started running around like they didn't have any sense, when Dev helped me in the car, I pulled my phone out and texted Ahmad.

Me: My water just broke, I'm omw to the hospital now

Stupid Nigga: That's what the fuck I'm talking about! I'll meet you up there.

I just chuckled and rested my head on the seat.

"Lord please don't let my family kill Ahmad" I had to say a silent prayer to myself, because I had a feeling that things are going to go bad tonight.
• •
"Oh my goodness, the babies are so adorable!" Dev's mama said.

"Thank you, auntie, they look just like their mama."

"You're so welcome baby, what are their names?"

"Amir Tyrone James, and Ashad Tyrone James."

"So, you did give them your father's name?" My auntie asked with teary eyes. I smiled just thinking about my daddy, if he was still alive, my sons would be spoiled rotten.

"You didn't even give them my last name Bianca?" Ahmad said while walking in. I'm not gone lie, even though I was mad that he is just now getting here he was standing there looking like a full course meal.

"Can yall please give us a minute?" I asked everybody that was in the room.

"Nah we can't give yall a minute," Dev said while holding the twins.

"Dev please," I whined. He laughed and handed me the twins before walking out with everybody.

"Damn Bianca, you just made my job so much easier," I looked at him confused.

"What are you talking about Ahmad?"

"Oh, you thought I was gone let you and that nigga live happily ever after? Then you had yo bitch ass brother jump me because you were out being a hoe, as soon as I kill those niggas and take over the business, I'm going to kill you and those lit-

70

tle angels." He tried to touch my babies, but I quickly snatched away, I can't believe Ahmad was acting like this.

"Ahmad please just leave." He walked over towards me and gave me a kiss that sent chills up my spine. This wasn't the same man that I knew. When he walked out the room, I laid my head back, held my babies close to me, and cried.

"Oh fuck no, Bianca what the fuck happened, why are you crying?" Kenyon asked me while taking my boys out of my hand.

"Yall were right, he said that he is going to kill yall, then me and my babies." When I burst out crying Kj automatically ran over towards me and hugged me tight.

"Best friend don't worry about any of that, you know we got you and those little niggas," Carter said trying to calm me down.

"That's the thing Carter, I'm not worried about myself; I'm worried about yall," I started to cry uncontrollably at the fact that my brother's lives are at risk.

"Hey, don't worry about us sis, we gone be alright," Kj said while kissing my forehead.

"POOH POOH!" Vonna screamed while running full force towards me. I carefully picked her up and kissed her cheek.

"Hey chunks, how did you get here?"

"My daddy," She pointed at Devin who was walking in.

"Where are the babies?"

"Uncle Kenyon is holding my baby's hostage, give me my babies Kenny."

"Man, as soon as I get these little niggas, you want them back." He handed them to me, and as soon as I had them in my arms Vonna started crying.

"What's wrong baby?" I asked concerned.

"You're they Mommy, but not mine." She pouted. Not knowing what to say next I looked at Dev for his, but he shrugged his shoulders.

"What are you talking about Davonna?" She wiped her face before responding.

"I want you to be my mommy because my Mommy is mean."

"You want me to be your mommy?" I asked feeling a mixture of joy but overwhelmed. She smiled and nodded.

"Okay baby I'll be your mommy, now wipe your face and stop crying." She clapped her hands and jumped in the bed with me, I kissed her cheek and watched as she played with her new brothers.

• •

One Month Later

"Bitch, yo best friend got me so fucked up right now." Ash said while walking in the door and grabbing Ashad.

"Will you please not cuss around my kids, what did Carter do now?"

"This nigga think he's slick, he is just now getting home from yesterday doing God know what, and the first think he do is get in the shower and wash his cheating ass dick!" She yelled obviously forgetting that he had to make a run last night.

"Girl calm yo ass down, did you forget that they had to go to the warehouse last night?" She stood there with this dumb ass look on her face then started laughing.

"Bitch I forgot, maybe I should go apologize for setting his car on fire."

"Tell me you didn't do that Ash?" Everybody know how Carter feel about his cars, so I know for a fact Ash is about to get her ass beat.

"Bitch you know I'm crazy, I sure in the fuck did set that bitch on fire, what's popping brother!" Ash said when Dev opened the front door.

"What's up sis, what's up lil niggas!" He grabbed the twins

and kissed them on the cheek before walking upstairs.

"Damn bitch he still not talking to you?" Ash asked.

"Nope, the only time he will is if it's about the kids, other than that, he stays out of my way and I stay out of his.

"Ashton where yo big head ass at!" We all turned around and saw Carter storming in the back door looking like he wanted to kill her. I looked at Ash and she had this smirk on her face like he wasn't about to kill her.

"Yes daddy, you called me?"

"Bitch don't daddy me, did you set my car on fire?"

"I sure did. What are you going to do about it?" She stood up and walked towards him.

"Bring yo psycho ass on before I fuck you up dude."

"You know I like that aggressive shit Papi," she grabbed his dick and walked outside. I just shook my head and went upstairs. When I walked in the room, I seen the twins in their bassinets and Dev in the bed sleep. I quickly took a shower and got in bed without putting any clothes on, making sure to scoot as far away from his grumpy ass. I could tell that this was going to be a sleepless night because for some reason I couldn't sleep without feeling his touch. After about thirty minutes of tossing and turning I scooted closer to him and laid my head on his chest.

"Get off me mama" Hearing him call me that brought a smile to my face, ever since he's been mad at me it was always Bianca.

"I don't want to; I can't sleep without being on you."

"Move B, I ain't fucking with you like that."

"Why not though, I don't understand," I tilted my head up to so I could look at him, but he had his eyes closed.

"Are you still fucking with that nigga Ahmad?"

"No, I'm not baby, you're the only nigga that I'm fucking

with," he opened his eyes and looked at me.

"Yea ah ight, tell me anything to make my heart skip a beat," He joked. I burst out laughing at his corny ass.

"Dev I'm being serious right now," I whined while bending down and kissing his lips. Feeling his dick get hard under me had my pussy throbbing, I bit my lips and started grinding against his dick.

"Nah shorty, don't even try it, you said that we have to wait until we make things official," I smacked my lips and laid back down.

"I know I said that, but I'm horny baby."

"Well take yo horny ass to sleep, you have to get your daughter in the morning."

"How come Uncle D can't drop her back off?" Vonna stayed at her grandparents' house for the weekend, because she said we were boring.

"He said that he was too tired to get up."

"I guess I'll go get her," I laid back down on his chest, and he started playing in my hair which instantly put me to sleep.

The next morning, I woke up to people jumping in my bed screaming, when I opened my eyes Vonna and Dev was jumping up and down on the bed while cracking up.

"Good morning Mommy!" Vonna yelled.

"Good morning chunks, stop jumping in the bed before you fall and bust yo head open," she flopped down on the bed and jumped on top of me. Dev's childish ass was still jumping on the bed, so I tripped him making him fall on the floor. Me and Vonna started cracking up after seeing his face when he fell.

"Oh, so yall thought that was funny, that's okay I got yall," he said when he got up off the floor.

"No baby I'm sorry, I didn't mean to laugh." I said trying to get on his good side, but it wasn't working.

"Nah I'm gone get yall back," he smirked then walked out the room.

"Vonna hand me my robe," when she gave it to me, I quickly put it on, grabbed Vonna and ran to her room. I looked in her toy box, grabbed her water gun, and went to her bathroom to fill them up with water.

"When you see daddy shoot him okay?" She laughed and nodded. I handed her the gun and was about to walk out but I had to figure out where my babies were.

"Where are your brothers?"

"Uncle Kenyon came and picked them up," I nodded then opened the door. Grabbing her hand, we walked downstairs and heard him on the phone.

"Bro just let me know what yall trying to do tonight, hold on Kj I think I'm about to kill yo sister and niece," Dev said with an evil smirk on his face. I looked at Vonna then nodded my head. On three we started spraying him with water, he tried to run after us but fell which caused Vonna to crack up laughing. I picked her up and ran in to the bathroom, locked the door and waited two minutes to go back in the kitchen to find Dev, when I didn't see him anywhere, I started to get scared cause I knew his ass was somewhere hiding.

"Devin where are you at, I'm not playing anymore," I said while looking around.

"Mommy he's behind you!" Vonna screamed while trying not to laugh, I quickly turned around and saw that he had to big water guns in his hand.

"Dev please don't get my hair wet," I cried

"Nah I don't want to hear any of that," he aimed the gun at me and started spraying us with water, for the next fifteen minutes we ran around the house spraying each other until we heard people coming in the house.

"Man, y'all some big ass kids, who the fuck runs around

with water guns, ole Radio looking ass mother fuckers," Kenyon said while sitting on the couch. Kayin, Kj, Carter, Ash, Davon, and that bitch Staci walked in.

"Kj keep yo dog on the leash while she's in my house, Dev pick yo wet ass daughter up off the floor, I swear this girl will fall asleep whenever she is," I said

"Why the fuck are yall here anyway?" Dev asked while picking her up off the floor.

"Shit we got bored and didn't have anything else to do," Kj said.

"We will be back after we change," we walked up the stairs and went inside my room.

"I'm about to go put some dry clothes on her and put her in the bed," he kissed my lips and walked out the room. I stripped out of my clothes and went to take a shower. After taking a shower and handling my hygiene. I walked out the bathroom to see Dev leaning on the wall putting some joggers on, I walked over to him and wrapped my arms around his waist. He bent down and pecked my lips while staring at me making me feel uncomfortable.

"Why are you just staring at me like a creep?"

"Because you are the most beautiful woman I have ever seen in my entire life," unable to look at him any longer I turned my head and blushed.

"Thank you daddy, you're not too bad looking yourself."

"You know I love you right?" When he said that my emotional ass looked at him trying not to cry.

"Really?"

"Yes really, ever since I met you, I couldn't help but notice how loyal and caring you were. You are amazing with Vonna, and today just made me love you even more. I have never had anybody who were like you, you're rude but friendly and that's what make me love you," not able to hold back the tears I laid my head on his chest and cried.

"I love you too daddy, you just made my entire day."

"Don't say that shit just because I said it mama, I want you to mean it," he said while looking at me.

"No, I really do mean it baby, I love you to death," he grabbed my face and kissed me passionately while laying me on the bed and kissed me from head to toe. He made sure to pay more attention to my stomach because he knows that I can be insecure about my weight sometimes, once he made it too my sweet spot, he parted my lips with his fingers and dived in headfirst.

"Oh, shit Dev wait," I moaned. He wrapped his arms around my waist to make sure that I didn't go anywhere. This man was sucking the soul out of my pussy, as soon as I felt his tongue inside of me, I knew I was about to cum.

"Fuck yes, oh God right there baby, I'm about to cum!" He started sucking on my clit and playing with my pussy, withing no time I released my juices all on him and he made sure to catch every drop. The sight of my juices dripping from his beard when he stood up had me wanting to feel him deep inside of me.

"Are you sure you're ready for this mama?" He asked. While nodding my head I spread my legs across the bed anticipating the feel of him being inside of me. He climbed on top of me and just looked me in my eyes.

"You're mine, fuck all that official shit, you're mine forever do you hear me?" I nodded my head and grabbed his face kissing him passionately. He took his time pushing himself inside of me, but once he was in there it was a mixture between pain and pleasure.

"Fuck yo pussy so fucking tight and wet mama damn," he groaned while burying his face between my neck. He started fucking me slow making sure to hit my spot every time, the way this man is making me feel is honestly indescribable, I have never felt like this before, he was taking his time with my body and I was loving every minute of it.

"Shit Devin hold on baby please I can't take it!" I tried to squirm away, but he held my hands above my head and started sucking on my neck.

"Where do you think you're going, look at me Bianca, no other nigga will make you feel the way I do. I am making love to your mind body and soul, do you hear me?" I couldn't speak so I just nodded my head. He started giving me these long deep strokes making me lose my breath.

"Do you hear me mama?"

"Fuck yes I hear you daddy!" I yelled. He started going faster and deeper making my eyes roll in the back of my head.

"Fuck daddy I'm about to cum," I started shaking uncontrollably and came so hard I couldn't breathe.

"Fuck," Dev grunted while spilling his seeds deep inside of me. He collapsed on the side of the bed and put his arm across his face. I got up and tried to walk to the bathroom so I could pee, took a quick shower and came back out with a warm towel so I can clean his dick off.

"Pussy so good I put his ass to sleep," I laughed while cleaning his dick off. I threw on a pair of black leggings and a T-shirt, then went downstairs.

"Where did everybody go?" I walked outside and saw everybody mugging me.

"What the fuck did I do?"

"You couldn't fucking wait until we left?" Kj asked

"Nah we couldn't actually," I laughed while walking over to Carter and sitting next to him.

"Best friend can we go out tomorrow I miss you."

"I don't care, just let me know when and where," Carter said while kissing my cheek.

"Yo why the fuck is this nigga still calling yo phone?" Dev asked while walking outside with my phone in his hand.

"I don't know Dev, I haven't talk to him since the twins were born," I shrugged and walked over to him.

"Answer it and see what he wants," he handed me my phone and I quickly answered before Ahmad hung up.

"Hello?"

"What's up baby mama."

"Ahmad what do you want?" He laughed at my attitude.

"You better get in the house if you don't want to die baby," he said then hung up.

"Go in the house, where is Vonna at?" Dev asked while grabbing me.

"She's still sleep and I'm not going anywhere," everybody got their guns out and waited, I ran in the house and woke Vonna up.

"Baby go get in the closet and don't come out until I tell you too okay?"

"Mommy you're scaring me," she started to cry which made me get mad. I can't believe that Ahmad is really acting like this. I gave her the iPad and headphone, then put her in the closet. The sound of gun fire brought me back to life, I grabbed one of Dev's guns that was in the closet and ran back outside.

"Noooo!" I screamed when I noticed that some man had his gun aimed at Kj's head. I ran towards him while making sure to pull the trigger killing the dude instantly. Once the car drove off, I saw that Sheila's boyfriend Richard was in the back seat with a smirk on his face.

"What the fuck was that Bianca, you could've gotten killed, are you fucking stupid?" Kj yelled while getting up.

"Kj if I didn't kill him you would've been dead, this is why I told you that I don't want y'all in the streets!" I yelled while hitting him in his head real hard.

"This shit has nothing to do with our business, this shit is yo fault," Kj yelled in my face.

"Bro chill out." Kayin said trying to calm Kj down.

"No Kayin it's coo, what's my fault Kj?" I asked clearly pissed.

"If you wouldn't have opened your legs to Killa and started acting like a hoe, Ahmad wouldn't of fucking left!" I couldn't do anything but look at him, did nigga just really say that?

"Watch what the fuck you say bro," Dev said in a calm tone while pulling me back, but I jerked away from him and looked at Kj.

"That's how you feel Kj? Let me explain something to you, Ahmad was beating my ass for a whole fucking year. He killed my fucking daughter Kj, him turning his back on us had nothing to do with me, he has been plotting on y'all since day one!" I screamed

"What are you talking about Bianca?" Carter asked.

"Last night he butt dialed me, I was gone hang up, but he started talking about how he set y'all up, and how hee was the one who robbed the traps. He said that him and his brothers was supposed to inherit the family business."

"Who the fuck is his brother?" Kayin asked.

"He didn't say, he just kept saying something about this person named God."

"Do you know who he was talking to?" Carter asked me.

"Some woman, but I did see Richard in the back seat of that truck," I said while looking at Dev letting him know that his bitch ain't shit.

"Sheila's boyfriend?" Dev asked.

"Yep."

"Go pack some clothes for you and Vonna," I kissed his lips and went upstairs to Vonna's room and pulled her out the closet.

"Are you okay baby?" She looked like she wasn't hurt but she was scared.

"Yes, Mommy I'm fine, what was that noise?"

"Don't worry about it baby, go get those clothes that's hanging up in our clothes and put them in the suitcase that's in the closet okay?" She nodded her head; I kissed her cheek walked in my room and cried.

"Knock knock, are you okay Pooh?" Carter asked while leaning on the door.

"Carter I can't believe that Kj said all of that to me, it came out of nowhere."

"I know Pooh, but you know that he didn't mean any of it, he was just pissed off at the moment."

"I understand that Carter, but it doesn't change that fact that it hurts, I was defending him, and if I wasn't there, he would've gotten killed."

"Come here." Carter demanded. I stood up and walked towards him. He pulled me in for a hug and held me tight.

"I understand what you were trying to do, but you have to understand that you made Kj feel weak when you shot that dude."

"I understand that it's an ego thing, but we all know that he shouldn't have said any of the shit that came out of his mouth Carter and you know it."

"Let's just drop it for right now, rock is on his way to come get you and Vonna, he stopped by Uncle D's house and got the twins already," he kissed my forehead and let me go.

"Where are we going?"

"To a hotel until we figure this shit out."

"Carter I'm scared," I admitted. I wasn't scared for me; I

was scared for my family.

"Everything will be okay Bianca, trust me," I gave him one more hug then went to go get Vonna out of her room and of course she was sleeping, Carter picked her up while I grabbed her suitcase and headed downstairs. Everyone was in the living room sitting down trying to figure out what the fuck just happened. Dev was sitting at the bar with a murderous look in his eyes, I walked towards him and stood in between his legs.

"Baby are you okay, you got that look in your eyes," he looked at me for ma moment before trying to smile, then pecked my lips.

"To be completely honest, no I'm not but I gotta get my head right so we can find that night Ahmad, you know we gone have to kill him, right?"

"Yes, I do, and I don't care, just be careful, and you better find that bitch Sheila before I do."

"I got you with yo gangsta ass," I just and kissed his lips. I already know that this is about to take up majority of his time but it's something that has to be done in order to save our family.

CHAPTER 11

Carter

"**K**j you have to be the dumbest nigga on earth!" I yelled in his face. Out of all of us I was the calmest and levelheaded one. It took a lot to piss me off, and this nigga here is about to make me beat his ass. Everybody know that I don't play when it comes to pooh, she is not only my best friend, she is my world.

"Carter get yo ass out my face dude, everybody in here know that I'm telling the truth. All of this shit is her fault, and somebody needed to tell her that," he said unfazed.

"Kj shut yo bitch ass up, ain't none of this bullshit that's going on my sisters' fault, she didn't know that he was plotting against us, that nigga had all of us fooled," Kenyon said clearly pissed off as well

"Whenever y'all bitches are done arguing, we need to figure out where this nigga Ahmad is, and what we are going to do," Killa said looking like he had the world on his shoulders.

"I think we need to talk to pops and Uncle D," Kj said

"Nigga for what, they don't know shit just like we don't, what we need to do is go talk to Sheila and her bitch ass boyfriend," I said looking directly at Killa. I understand that he is in a bad situation right now, but I really don't give a fuck, that bitch knows something About Ahmad and his crew.

"Let's just go over there now, I could give two fucks about the bitch." Killa said while walking out the house Surprising all of us. Killa always said that no matter what goes on he would never physically hurt Sheila because she is the mother of his child, but I guess shit change. I pulled my ringing phone out my pocket and answered it.

"What's up baby? I'm busy right now."

"Carter what the fuck is going on, Pooh just called me crying saying that Kj went off on her because she was trying to save his life," Ash yelled.

"Don't worry about it baby, we got it under control, I'm about to send you the address, pack some shit and go up there with her." I said calmly.

"Why the fuck are you always so damn calm, that shit irritates my soul, ole mellow head ass." She yelled. Everybody hates that I'm always so calm and chilled about every, but I can't help it. Ever since I was young, always quiet and didn't let shit get to me. I feel like it takes more energy on stressing about shit you can't fix, I always been anti-social and hate being around a big crowd for a long period of time.

"Ash please just shut the fuck up and do as I say."

"Yo ass better be lucky you got some good dick," before I could respond her crazy ass hung up, I just shook my head and got in the car.

• •

"Sheila open this fucking door right now!" Killa said while banging on the door.

"Bro chill before her nosey ass neighbors come out here," Davon said trying to get his brother to calm down.

"Devin why are you banging on my damn door like that?" Sheila asked while swinging the doors open. As soon as she saw us standing there her eyes got big and she began to cry.

"Killa I'm so sorry, I didn't want to set you up but Ahmad and Richard force me to," she began to cry uncontrollably and beg for his forgiving, but it was falling on deaf ears. I looked on the side of her house and see Ahmad climbing out of the window trying to get away, I calmly pulled out my gun and shot him in the leg.

"Carter what the fuck dude!" Kj yelled while pulling out his gun.

"Ahmad was climbing out of the window, so I shot him in the leg," I said nonchalantly like it wasn't a big deal. Kenyon and Davon burst out laughing which caused me to laugh as well.

"Yo I can't stand this funny looking nigga, he is so fucking relaxed after he just shot somebody, I wanna be like you when I grow up." Davon said while following everyone towards Ahmad. Killa still had Sheila by her hair while her dramatic ass screamed.

"Damn Carter you're supposed to be my brother, and this is how you treat me, you gone shoot me in my leg?" Ahmad said wit me a smirk on his face, I shrugged my shoulders and leaned on the wall.

"I guess you can't trust everybody can you?" I said never taking my eyes off of him.

"Ahmad what the fuck is wrong with you dude, what made you want to turn your back on us?" Kj asked sounding hurt.

"Y'all are what's wrong with me, walking around here like y'all shit don't stank," he answered sound like a bitch. Tired of hearing all this talking and heart felt shit, I shot Ahmad in his other leg and walked away.

"Where are you going bro, are you good?" Kayin asked.

"I'm good bro, tell Kj not to kill him yet, bring him to the warehouse." Kayin nodded and walked back to the side of the house.

Later on at the warehouse

"What made you turn your back on us Ahmad?" Kenyon asked.

"God," je simply replied.

"Who the fuck is God Ahmad?" Kj asked

"My brother."

"I'm gone need you to stop acting like a bitch and answer the question right," Davon said sounding irritated.

"Nigga fuck you, what makes you think I'm gone tell y'all niggas anything? Y'all gone kill me anyways, so I might as well keep my mouth shut, y'all will find out sooner or later, I just wish I could've sampled Pooh's sweet pussy one last time," when he said that Killa walked over to Ahmad and started beating him until he was barely breathing. Ahmad spit blood from his mouth and laughed.

"I guess it's true what people say, keep your friends close and enemies closer." When he said that I took one last pull from the blunt I was smoking and walked over to him. I looked at my brother's and waited for them to let me know when they were ready. When they all nodded their heads, I aimed my gun at Ahmad and shot him twice in the chest.

"I'll call up the cleanup crew," I responded never taking my eyes off Ahmad, they all nodded and walked out the warehouse without saying another word. I took one last look at Ahmad then followed behind my brother's.

CHAPTER 12

Killa

"Fuck, I forgot we had that bitch in the trunk," Kj said referring to Sheila.

"I got her bro, y'all go home and chill, and I'll meet up with y'all," they all nodded and drove off. I got in my car and drove to my condo that nobody knew I had. Once I made it there, I got her out the trunk and forced her in the house.

"Killa please don't do this I'm so sorry," she begged. I pulled the blunt that I rolled up earlier out my pocket and lit it up.

"You might as well shut the fuck up, where yo man at Sheila?"

"I don't know Devin I promise."

"You do realize you could've killed your fucking daughter right; did you even think about her for a second?"

"But she didn't get hurt Devin, I told them not to hit her," I looked at her like she was crazy.

"She's your fucking daughter Sheila, you gave birth to her!"

"Not anymore, it's always been about Davonna, you never cared about me, did you? I knew I should've let Richard kill her like he wanted to," she thought she mumbled the last part, but I heard every word. With no hesitation I shot her in the head and watch her limp body fall to the ground. I picked up my phone and called Rock.

"yo," he answered

"What's up Nigga, mama said bring her a loaf of bread," I

said talking in code.

"How many?"

"Just one loaf."

"Ah ight I'll be on my way," I hung up the phone and walked out the house never looking back. Today has been a crazy day, I went from playing with my family, to getting shot at, then killing two people I just want to go back to the hotel and chill with my family.

. . . .

As soon as I walk in the hotel room B jumped up from the couch and ran towards me.

"Oh my God baby are you okay, where did all this blood come from? LORDT somebody hurt my baby!" Her extra ass screamed. I couldn't do anything but stand there and laughed at her dramatic ass.

"Will you sit yo crazy ass down somewhere Bianca, this is not my blood so chill out crazy." I walked in the bathroom, stripped out of my clothes, and got in the shower, after I was done, I went back in the room with a towel wrapped around my waist not knowing that we had company.

"Damn bitch yo nigga came out here looking like an old spice commercial and shit." Ash said while laughing., both of them are characters when they get together.

"Bitch get yo silly ass out of here before I fuck you up for looking at my nigga." B warned but Ash laughed and kissed her on the cheek before walking out the door.

"Come here Daddy," B said while holding her arms out waiting for me, I gladly walked over to her stretching out so that my head was in her lap.

"So, who's blood was that on you, Ahmad's?"

"No, Carter killed him," she looked at me confused.

"Then who?"

"Sheila's," I said without opening my eyes.

"Yass, I thought I was gonna have to kill her myself," she bent down and kiss my lips with so much passion that I instantly bricked up, I was about to play with her pussy but I just realized I haven't seen my kids.

"Where my kids at?" I asked.

"Kenyon kidnapped them for the night."

"Damn, I haven't seen my babies all day, baby hand me my phone." She picked up my ringing phone, looked at the number then rolled her eyes. When she handed me my phone, I realize it was Kj.

"What's up Kj?"

"Pops and Uncle D said they want to meet up with us tonight."

"Man, what the fuck for?" I looked at B and she rolled her eyes then got up.

"I don't fucking know Killa, just bring your ass!"

"Man, ight I'll be there, I said then hung up the phone.

"Come on crazy, you're going with me," her happy ass jumped up and threw on some clothes.

"Bring yo ass on B, I don't wanna be here all night."

"I'm coming nigga damn!" She ran out the bathroom and jumped on my back.

"Get yo silly ass off of me Bianca."

"Nope I'm fine up here," she kissed my cheek and laid her head on my shoulder. This is what I love about her, she always know how to put a smile on my face even when I'm not in a good mood. She always find joy out of a bad situation; this woman is my rock.

"Y'all kids can never be serious can y'all?" Kenyon said while struggling to carry both car seats. We all decided to check in too a hotel just in case some shit goes down.

"Nigga if you drop my babies, I'm gone fuck yo Scooby Doo looking ass up." B said in a serious tone.

"Shut the fuck up ole Ms. Trunchbull looking ass." Kenyon said while handing me one of the car seats.

"Kenyon, who the fuck is that?" Kayin asked.

"That teaching bitch from Matilda, y'all dummies know who I'm taking about," we all looked at him confused.

"Oh my God, the big one who threw the black girl around, and locked Matilda up in that closet thing." B said trying not to laugh. Once we figured out who he was talking about, we all started cracking up laughing.

"Will you please shut the fuck up and come on with yo stupid ass." I laughed and walked away. Only Kenyon would say some shit like that.

"Daddy can I ride with Uncle Kenyon?" Vonna asked while running towards me.

"Yea baby go ahead," B said before I could answer. She know I hates when she gives Vonna anything she wants. I strapped my babies in and got in the car.

"You gone have to stop telling her yes to everything that she ask for Bianca. That's why her ass is spoiled now," I said as soon as she got in the car. She looked at me like I just offended her.

"But that's my baby D, she can get anything she wants," I looked at her then drove off.

"That's why she acts like that Bianca cause you give her everything, you gone have to stop that shit," she licked her lips then smiled.

"You're looking good as fuck right now daddy, SMACK-ABLE!"

"Don't try to change the subject Bianca, you heard what I said," Ignoring me, She unbuckled her seatbelt, leaned over and started kissing on my neck. Her freaky ass know that's my weak spot. She started to unbuckle my pants while massaging my dick.

"B whhat the fuck are you doing ma?" She smirked then deep throated my dick in one motion.

"Shit mama fuck!" Not being able to control the wheel anymore I pull over on the side of the road and started fucking her face. The wetness of her mouth, the way she was massaging my balls, and her deep throating my dick had be ready to bust.

"Fuck, watch out mama I'm about to nut," when I said that, she started going faster, and in no time I was spilling my seeds down her throat.

"Damn ma, yo head is lethal," she smirked while cleaning off my dick. Once she was done, I drove off on cloud nine.

"What the fuck took yo ass so long?" Kj started bitching as soon as we walked in the door. He couldn't even mess up the good ass mood I was in, I just got some fire ass head, and I'm gone get some pussy as soon as we get back to the room.

"I ain't gone lie, I got some cuddy last night," I said just to fuck with him.

"Dude bring yo ass on," he smacked me in the back of my head and walked in to my Unc's office.

"What's up pops, Unc."

"What's going on son, have a seat so we can get started," I sat in the chair next to Davon and snatched the blunt out his hand.

"So what's going on, why did y'all call us here?" I asked getting straight to the point.

"Why did we have to find out that Ahmad was a snake?" My uncle asked

"Because as soon as we would've told y'all, we would be sitting shot gun while y'all took over, we handled it ourselves pops." Kj explained.

"Did y'all, cause from what I hear he has a brother named God and y'all don't know who that is, then Rock told us that y'all dumb asses got shot at today," my pops said while looking at me and Davon. Don't get me wrong, my pop's is an OG, but that nigga don't put fear in my heart.

"We did get shot at, but once again we handled it. Every time something goes bad y'all can't turn in to super dads and shit, let us handle this, we gone figure out who this God person is, damn y'all need to sit y'all old asses down somewhere," Kenyon said clearly annoyed.

"Yea ah ight, we gone give y'all time to handle this. Did y'all ever ask Ash if she knew anything about Ahmad having a brother?" We all looked at each other confused when my Unc said that.

"Why would Ash know anything Ahmad pops?" Carter asked.

"They used to mess around before him and Pooh got together, y'all didn't know this?" Unc said looking confused.

"He'll nah we didn't fucking know this, sis a fucking snake too?" Kj said furious.

"We are about to find out," Carter said while getting up.

"Somebody go get him before he kill that girl!" my pops said while getting up. For Ash's sake I hope that Unc is wrong.

CHAPTER 13

Ashton

"Girl I can't believe Ahmad would do this to our family," I rolled my eyes and ignored Pooh's comment about Ahmad. Truth be told I'm glad his El DeBarge looking ass is dead

"Bitch if you don't shut yo ass up about him, NOBODY CARES!"

"You're right girl, so what's been going on with you and Carter, are y'all good?" She asked. Just thinking about him had my pussy wet, and my heart fluttering. Besides my daughter, Carter is the best thing that has ever happened to me.

"Ash where yo hoe ass at!" Carter yelled while running down the hall. Ever since I been with him, I have never heard him yell, or even get mad. I quickly got up and tried to run, but he pulled me by my hair and yanked me back.

"Carter what the fuck, let her go!" Pooh yelled while trying to get him off of me. He pushed her so hard she hit her head on the wall.

"Bitch you was fucking Ahmad?" When he asked me that my heart dropped in my stomach.

"Carter no, I wouldn't do that to Pooh!" I screamed trying to sound believable.

"What is he talking about Ash, why would he say that?" Pooh asked confused.

"Tell her bae, tell your best friend how you was fucking her man behind her back," Carter yelled with his gun now aimed at my face.

"WHAT, Ash please tell my he's lying," When I looked at my best friend's face, she had tears in her eyes.

"Bianca I'm sorry, I didn't mean for any of this to happen," I cried

"How long were y'all fucking?" Carter asked.

"Carter please," I begged.

"How long!" Pooh yelled now standing next to Carter.

"We started two months before y'all got together, and a year after...." I started talking and cried uncontrollably.

"After what Ashton!" Pooh yelled.

"Bianca please," she grabbed the gun from Carter and put it against my temple.

"Yo sis chill out," Kayin tried to take the gun from her, but she snatched away.

"After what?" She asked calmly.

"After um.. Aubree was born." I whispered then put my head down. She dropped the gun and looked at me.

"Wait, so you was messing with him when we were together, and he's the father of your baby?" I nodded my head and looked away.

"Yes he is.' I said looking at Pooh.

"Wow I can't believe you would do this to me," Pooh cried while walking out the door. The look in her eyes cut me so deep, I didn't want to live anymore. The fact that I lost my best friend, and the only man I love hurt so bad.

"Get up Ash," Kj said with no expression on his face. I looked at Carter and saw that he was staring at me with a look of disgust. I quickly got up and followed everybody outside.

"I'll meet yall niggas at the warehouse, I'm about to take B and the kids back to the room," Killa said then jogging to the car. I looked Pooh, and she was staring at me with hate in her eyes. I never knew what alone felt like until I lost the two most important people in my life.

CHAPTER 14

Carter

"Carter are you good bro?" Kj asked, I just ignored him and continued to drive to the warehouse. I couldn't get the fact that Ash actually fucked around with Ahmad behinds Pooh's back and had a baby with him. I know I did a lot of foul shit in the past, but I never wanted to hurt my family. Watching my best friend break down in front of me was the hardest thing that I ever had to do.

"Bro you're ready for this shit?" Kj asked causing me to jump back into reality. I got out the car and made my way in the warehouse, I sat down directly in front of Ash and just stared at her.

"I'm gone ask you this only one time, and you better not lie. Do you know anything about Ahmad?" I asked getting straight to the point.

"No I don't, we never talked about his personal life, all we talked about was how much we were hurting Pooh. I would never do anything to hurt yall." She said honestly. Even though I didn't want to believe her, I couldn't help it. I knew for a fact she was telling the truth.

"I want you to pack all yo shit and stay the fuck away from my family, don't even try to contact me or Pooh and I mean that shit," I said then walked away, I didn't even wanna hear anything she had to say.

By the time I made it home Ash had already been there and packed all of her things, when I left the warehouse I decided not to go straight home, so I went to paradise to clear my head.

When I walked in the guest room I saw Pooh and my God kids in the bed knocked out. I grabbed Ashad and Amir and put them in their basinets that I got for them cause Pooh was sleeping wild as fuck.

"Wake up Pooh," I softly shook her and waited for her to wake up. She opened her eyes and smiled at me.

"What's up Carter," she yawned and sat up.

"Come make me something to eat," I demanded, without any hesitation she got up and walked out the room. When Pooh feelings get hurt, she is usually nice to everyone, which I thought was backwards until I realized she wasn't normal.

"Burgers and fries?" She asked while opening the refrigerator.

"That's sounds good best friend."

"Did you kill her?"

"Nah I just told her to leave," she nodded and continued to make burgers.

"Do you wanna talk about it?" She asked.

"Nah I just want to chill and watch a movie with you."

"I almost thought you forgot about me; it seems like we haven't hung out in forever."

"Don't even try it, ever since you and Killa started fucking around, you stop fucking with the kid," I told her honestly, she put the burgers on the grill and sat on the counter.

"Well I'm here now, honestly the reason I stopped coming around is because I thought you replaced little ole me."

"With who Bianca?"

"Lil Boosie," She said trying not to laugh.

"Yo ass is crazy dude, you know damn well she doesn't look like Lil Boosie."

"Yes she do with her ugly ass."

"Something is seriously wrong with you Bianca, real shit

though, Staci is mad cool, I knew her before I met yall, but her parents made her move away, so that's why she left. I wouldn't lie to you Bianca."

"Mmm I guess, but I still don't like her raggedy ass."

"Bianca you can't be overprotective of me all the time, everybody in the whole fucking world know that I'm yo best friend. Yall gone have to talk eventually since her and Kj are fucking around pretty heavy," she looked at me then rolled her eyes.

"That's not my problem Carter."

"You can be so fucking stubborn sometimes."

"But you love me though," She stuck her tongue out at me then finished cooking. I sighed then walked in the living room and called Kayin.

"Yo what's up nigga," he answered, surprisingly in a good mood.

"You busy bro?"

"Nah what's up Carter, what's on yo mind?" I looked behind me making sure Pooh was not listening.

"Yo fucking sister man," I said while running my hands down my head.

"What about her, is she good?"

"She good man, calm yo ass down, I think I'm feeling her Kayin."

"Carter what the fuck bro," He groaned sounding like he was about to start yelling.

"Man I know I know, I been feeling like this for months now, and I don't know what to do."

"I honestly don't know what to say, this is a fucking problem waiting to happen."

"You don't think I know that, help me out bro." I complained.

"Carter come get yo food negro, and who were you talking to?" Pooh yelled from the kitchen, I quickly hung up the phone and went in the kitchen.

"Damn why are you so nosey shorty, I don't be all up in yo phone when you're talking to Killa."

"When we spend time together you already know that it is a no phone rule, now give it here Mr," I shook my head and gave her my phone.

"Thank you sir, you're mine for the night, now come sit down and eat." She kissed my cheek and walked to the table with our plated.

"Lord I need to get this girl out of my head," I said to myself. Me having feelings for Pooh is not something I want, but it's obviously out of my league.

CHAPTER 15

Pooh

Two Months Later

"Devin I wanna go do something today," I whined while trying to wake him up.

"Bianca if you touch me one more time, I'm gone fuck you up now move and go play with the kids," he said never opening up his eyes. I got out the bed and went downstairs in to the living room, Vonna was on the couch watching tv with the twins.

"Wanna go get our hair and nails done today Chunks?"

"Yes, can Auntie Ash come to?" She asked not knowing that Ash is no longer apart of the family.

"Um, Auntie Ash is not feeling well today baby, you don't wanna hang out with mommy today?"

"Yes, I do silly head, but can we at least take daddy with us?"

"Let's go wake him up," we both ran upstairs in my room and saw that he was knocked out on my side of the bed.

"Daddy Daddy wake up!" Vonna screamed while jumping on the bed.

"Davonna please stop jumping on the bed daddy is tired," he opened his eyes and looked at her.

"I just wanted you to go with me and mommy."

"Where are yall going Bianca?"

"Probably to your shop to get our hair and nails done," I shrugged.

"Ah ight, I'll have Rock follow yall there," I frowned at his response. Ever since Ahmad got killed, he has been overprotective of us and it's starting to get irritating.

"Why can't you go with us, you're always throwing us on someone else." I asked sounding frustrated.

"B please don't start, I'm too tired to argue with you, I'm not going, so Rock is going to make sure that yall get there," he said with authority.

"Yea okay, tell Rock to give me like two hours, come on Chunks lets go find you something to wear," I grabbed her hand and left out the room before I had to cuss him out. I picked Vonna out a pair of bleached Jeans, a white V-neck, and some all-white huaraches. I gave her a bath and helped her put her clothes on.

"Go downstairs and watch Tv until Uncle Rock gets here," she nodded and skipped downstairs. I went back in the room and took a quick shower. Once I was in the shower, I let the tears fall as I thought about Ashton. I can't believe she would do something like that to me. Not only did she hurt me, she hurt my best friend Carter. Once I was done in the shower I went back in my room and put lotion on my body.

"What time are you gone be back B?" I ignored his question and continued to put lotion on.

"Oh, so you don't hear me talking to you Bianca?"

"Devin will you please stop talking to me?" He was really starting to irritate me right now. He pulled me by my hair and made me straddle his lap.

"What's yo problem now mama?"

"You really don't know what my problem is? Lately you have been acting like you don't have time for us anymore," I pouted.

"You know me, and your brothers have been super busy lately. This is the only day I got off and I really just wanna stay in and rest," I understood where he was coming from, but I honestly didn't care.

"Well maybe if you would spend more time with your family other than being in the streets twenty-four fucking seven, we wouldn't be having these problems," after I said that I got up and went to the closet to put some clothes on.

"Mommy Uncle Rock is here!" Vonna said while bursting in the door.

"Here I come baby, go give yo daddy a hug and a kiss good-bye," she jumped on the bed and showered him with kisses before running out the room.

"Can daddy have a kiss from mama bear?" Dev asked playfully while getting up and walking towards me. I quickly grabbed my things and walked out the door ignoring his ignorant ass. When I made it downstairs, Rock was in my kitchen eating my damn food. Rock wasn't just one of my brother's workers he was like family, he's been around ever since I was about sixteen, and he honestly fits right in with all of us.

"Get out my kitchen Roderick!"

"Chill out with my Government name nigga, are the twins going or just yall two?" He took a bite of his sandwich then looked at me waiting for my response.

"Nah they are staying with their daddy today, bring yo ass on fixing big ass sandwiches and shit." I walked out the kitchen, and outside to help Vonna in the car. Rock fat ass came out to the car five minutes later with another sandwich in his hand.

"Why haven't you talked to your brother Bianca?" Rocked asked as soon as we pulled off.

"What am I talking to him for Rock?"

"That's your fucking brother Pooh, I understand that you are still in your feelings about what happened, but you have to realize that life is too short, stop being so fucking stubborn and talk to that man, he has been acting crazy ever since yall stop talking," once I realized how serious he was I burst out laughing. Rock was like a mini Kenyon, he was never serious, he was the type of person who would piss you off because they take everything as a joke. So, to hear him actually truing to be serious was funny as fuck.

"Nigga when did you become so serious?"

"What do you mean Wesley, I'm always serious."

"Who the fuck is Wesley Rock?"

"Wesley Snipes, you know that's your daddy." See what I'm talking about? His ass is so ignorant. One we made it to the shop it was packed just like I expected.

"Welcome to Lowe's Brother's Barber and Beauty Shop how can I help you?" The receptionist said never taking her eyes off of the computer screen.

"Is Toy here today?"

"Oh yes ma'am, she's in the back with a client," I nodded my head and took a seat at her desk. Vonna automatically sat with the nail tech and got her nails painted. I pulled out my phone and saw that I had a message from an unknown number.

678-555-1920: You better spend all the time you can with you family before it's too late.

I ain't gone lie, that message kind of had me shook, instead of telling Killa about it I'm just gone ignore it and block the number.

"Bitch why the fuck are you sitting there acting like this ain't yo niggas shop? Bring yo ass back here and keep me company, what's up eyes?" Toy crazy ass said. The reason why she called Rock eyes is because he had really pretty blue eyes that would make any bitch fall for him.

"Toy take yo bum booty ass on somewhere, I'm not playing with you today," Rock said with a smirk on his face.

"Lord please don't start yall two, Toy come on," I snatched her hand and walked to the back. Her client was under the dryer, so she decided to get started on my hair.

"So what's been going on in your life my love?" Toy asked me.

"Girl too much, I need a break from my family, it's like something new is going on every day with us. What's been going on with you?" I asked her which caused her to laugh and shake her head.

"Girl nothing at all, you know I have no life outside of this place besides my drunk of a mother, but I'll get into that later. Anyways I have to tell you something, but you have to promise me that you won't get mad," when she said that I turned around and just looked at her waiting for her to say what she has to say.

"Ashton came by here today," hearing that bitches name had me seeing red and ready to blow her fucking brains out.

"What the fuck did her snake ass want?"

"She just came to get her hair done, boo yall really need to talk, when I saw her today she looked a hot mess. I know what she did was completely wrong, but yall are best friends, you need to talk to her Bianca." Everybody keeps telling me that I need to talk to her, but I honestly can't bring myself up to it. I love my sister to death, but what she did really cross the line and I don't know if I could ever forgive her for it.

"Toy I will eventually talk to her, but I can't right now because I might kill her," there was a knock at the door that made both of us jump.

"Who the fuck is it banging on my damn door like that?" Toy yelled clearly irritated.

"I hope you don't talk to our employees like that Toya." Dev said while walking in. He tried to bend down and give me a kiss, but I turned my head which caused Toy to stick me with the needle.

"Stop fucking playing with me mama, Toy hurry up with her nappy ass head I need some pussy now," he said then walked out. I just shook my head and let her finish, even when I was mad at his big head ass, he always found a way to make my kitty tingle. Once she was done with my head we went back in the front of the shop, Vonna was sitting in Kayin's lap with his phone in his hand. Kj was standing by the door leaning on the wall. Deciding to get the conversation over with, I walked over to him and wrapped my arms around his waist.

"Kj I don't wanna fight anymore, I don't apologize for what I did, because I will do it again if I have to, but I do apologize for making you feel weak, and less of a man, that was never my intention." He just looked at me with no expression on his face which caused me to smack my lips.

"I know what I said hurt you, but I just want you to know that I meant some of the shit I said. No, it's not your fault that Ahmad decided to go against us, because it obvious that you didn't know, but I do think that yall break up and something to do with him losing his mind, and cause him to not think straight. If I hurt you in any kind of way I sincerely apologize." He said while looking me in my eyes which made me feel like a little girl.

"Sooooo are we coo?" I asked Impatiently. He looked at me with a smirk on his face.

"You and Staci need to talk, we are kicking it pretty heavy, and I need my two favorite girls besides Vonna to get along," I let go of him and rolled my eyes.

"Lordt you're asking for way too much buddy, I'll talk to her stanky ass just for you brother." I said causing him to laugh. He kissed me cheek then hugged me tightly.

"Yo we gotta go to the hospital now, Carter has been in a bad car accident!" Rock yelled while getting up and running out the door. All of a sudden I froze, I couldn't move even if I wanted to. Hearing that my best friend was in an accident felt like a real bad dream. If something happens to my best friend all hell is going to break lose.

CHAPTER 16

Kj

T he ride to the hospital was long and cold, I'm not the most spiritual person in the world, but right now I was praying that my brother would make it out of this. Once we made it to the hospital, we all went to the nurse's station to find Carter.

"Excuse me, I'm here for Carter Jenkins," I said speaking calmly. The nurse looked at me with a lustful stare.

"Can I have your name and number please?" She asked not even paying attention to Bianca who was ready to kill her.

"Listen here bitch, I'm not in the mood to play games with you. Do you have any information Carter or not?" Pooh said while getting in her face. The nurse smacked her lips then rolled her eyes.

"He was just brought in an hour ago, a doctor will be with the family shortly," she said with an attitude. We all went in the waiting room and sat down.

"Baby I'm sure Carter is going to be okay," Staci said while rubbing my back. I looked at Pooh and saw that she was in a daze curled up next to Killa, I know that if Carter don't make it through this, she is going to lose her mind.

"What happened to Carter yall, please tell me that he is okay!" We all turned around and saw Ash walking in with her daughter, and all of our parents.

"Ashton please just leave; we don't want any more problems," Kayin begged trying to get her to leave before Pooh go crazy.

"No Kayin I will not leave, I care about Carter just like everybody else in here," She sat by Uncle D and laid her head on his should, Pooh just stared at Ash's daughter without speaking.

"Let her stay," Pooh whispered, we all looked at her shocked at what she just said.

"Are you sure Bianca?" I asked making sure I heard her right. She nodded her head yes and closed her eyes.

"Bro she's too calm for me." I whispered to Kenyon, he just shook his head and nodded.

"Calm before the storm bro, you know Pooh ass is crazy as fuck, I'm honestly scared as fuck right now," I nodded my head in agreement.

"The family of Carter Jenkins," we all got up and walked towards the doctor.

"Carter had a lot of internal bleeding; he also had a significant amount of Hydrocodone's in his system. Thankfully we were able to pump his stomach in time, but right now its touch and go. The next twenty-four hours will be crucial for Carter." The doctor touched my shoulder then walked away, the thought that I might lose my brother tonight came to my head and I lost it.

"Fuck, I can't lose my brother man, I just can't!" I said while punching the wall and breaking down, never in my life have I ever cried in front of people, but I didn't care at this moment. My brother is laying in a hospital bed fighting for his life, Pooh ran over to me and held me tight until I was able to calm down.

"It's going to be okay Kj I promise, Carter is going to fight through this I know he is. He can't just leave us he just can't." Just hearing my sister soft voice calmed me down. It's amazing how she can be so strong some time.

"Oh my God we can't lose him," Ash cried. Pooh let go of me and started laughing which was a clear sign that my sister is about to black out.

"Bitch I know yo snake ass ain't crying," Bianca said while walking towards Ash.

"Bianca sit yo ass down right now, there are kids in here!" Our pops yelled.

"No, I'm not about to sit down daddy this bitch needs to leave. Every time I see you, I'm gone beat yo ass, every day that I can't talk to my bestfriend that's a bullet with your name on it, and every time I look at your child and I'm not able to look at my daughter, I'm gone beat that ass," Pooh said while trying to get to Ash

"You need to chill out with all them threats Pooh," Davon said while getting up and grabbing Ash which caused all of us to look at him.

"Yo bro chill out, I got this one over here." Killa said while getting in his brother's face.

"Nah it's okay baby, I got it, you see brother, I don't make threats, I will drop you and that bitch in a heartbeat. While you're over here worried about what's coming out of my mouth you need to worry about her sneaky pussy ass," Pooh said with a crazy ass look on her face. I grabbed her shoulder and looked at her.

"Chill out sis, she not even worth it."

"I'm tired of yo shit Bianca, Ahmad told me all about those days where you were too busy with Carter you couldn't be a mom to your daughter, all those late nights while you was gone I was taking care of her. That's when he started questioning if he was the father or not, maybe if you were a better mom to your kid she would still be alive." As soon as those words flew out of her mouth a look of guilt and regret came up on her face. At that moment everybody got up and tried to stop Pooh from literally killing Ash in this hospital.

"Let me go, bitch I'm gone kill you, I hate you Ashton, you

are my bestfriend, my fucking sister, and that's how you feel, get off of me, please let me go Kj, Kayin please, Kenyon please let me go, Devin tell them to let me go!" She was crying and trying to get out of our grip, but we wouldn't let her. The last time I seen her like this was when she lost her first daughter, it hurts my heart to see my sister this hurt.

• •

Shit is fucked up without my brother, it's been two weeks and he still is in a coma. Each and every one of our trusted workers has been up here to check on him, the streets are not the same without my right hand by my side.

"Pooh you gotta eat something sis," I said to Pooh, but like always she just ignored me. She has been sitting in the same spot since Carter came to the hospital, she hasn't spoken to anyone or even ate. She just sat there and stared at Carter. It breaks my heart knowing that my sister is hurting. I wish there was something I could do to take this pain away.

"Hey baby are you hungry?" Staci came in the room and kissed my cheek.

"Yea bring me some Chinese food."

"Should I bring Pooh something?" She asked while looking at Pooh.

"Nah I'll give her some of mine," she nodded then walked out.

"What's up son," my pops said while walking in with my brothers.

"Hey pops, what's up yall." My pops walked over to Pooh and hugged her.

"How is he holding up?"

"The same, they said if they do not see any improvement, they are going to take him off of life support," when I said that Pooh's head popped up and she looked at me.

"What, why didn't you say anything to me Kj," Pooh said while crying

"I'm sorry sis, I tried to tell you, but you wasn't listening."

"No, you should of told me, Carter wake up, best friend wake up please, I can't do this without you, I need you, best-friend please wake up! You have to fight this, don't die please don't die!" Pooh fell on the floor and sobbed Uncontrollably. My pops walked out cause he couldn't stand to see Pooh like this. I just grabbed her of the floor and rocked her until she was able to catch her breath. All of a sudden Carter's monitors started beeping like crazy and he started having a seizure, the doctor's rushed in and put Pooh and I out.

"Kj what just happened?" Pooh whispered.

"I don't know sis, I don't know," I pulled her towards me and let her cry until she couldn't anymore.

"Lord if you pull my brother out of this, I promise I'll do right and stay out of the street," I said out loud. Pooh wiped her face and looked at me.

"You better mean that shit Ka'Mari."

"I do sis, come on let's wait on the doctors to come out," I grabbed her hand and lead her into the lobby. I have a feeling we are about to see what life is like without my nigga in it.

CHAPTER 17

Carter

When I heard Pooh crying, I tried my hardest to wake up, I tried to fight but I couldn't. I wanted to hold her and let her know that I'm okay, but something inside of me was giving up, so I just stopped fighting. I couldn't fight anymore; this was my fate. God was punishing me for all of the wrong I did, and the wrong that I was going to do in the future. I didn't expect for any of this to happen, I was just so pissed at what I walked in on I blacked out. A couple weeks before my accident Ash came to me begging to take her back, I can't lie and say I didn't miss her because I did, and I decided to give her another try. A week later I decided to pop up at the hotel that she was staying at so I could take her out on a date, I made my way inside and saw her giving head to Davon, once I saw that I got pissed the fuck off and left.

Once I got home, I just sat on the bed and thought about what I just saw, I had a headache just thinking about the bull shit so I went downstairs to the kitchen and took a hydrocodone then washed it down with a bottle of Henny. After I took the pill I was about to walk back up to my room when I saw some mail on the counter for her, against my better judgment I opened the mail and saw that it was papers from the abortion clinic. When I seen that she killed my seed I black out and stop thinking straight, Ash knew how bad I wanted kids, and the fact that she had an abortion made me want to kill her. I grabbed the bottle of pills and took some more and left forgetting that I already took one in the kitchen, I started feeling dizzy so I tried to pull over to collect my thoughts, but I lost control of the wheel and the car flipped over and everything went black, and that's the last thing I remember.

So here I am fighting for my life so I can wake up and tell Pooh and Kj that I'm okay, but I couldn't I felt my body giving up. I just hope God forgive me for my sins. I just stopped fighting and gave up; I had a good life I just wish I could apologize to my family for the wrong I done.

CHAPTER 18

Ashton

"Can you hurry the fuck up and get yo shit so we can get out of here Ash!" Davon yelled in my ear for the hundredth time. I know fucking with him is wrong, but I couldn't help myself. It was something about Davon that made me want him more, just thinking about the first time we actually talked had me blushing.

One Month ago

"Mommy can I get this one please, I promise not to ask for anything else," My daughter screamed while throwing more toys in the basket. I know Carter told me to stay away from the family, but I just couldn't do that. I love him too much to let something like this get in the middle of our relationship, so I asked Pooh's daddy if I could stay in the condo that he has. Just thinking about Pooh brought tears to my eyes. Never in a million years have I ever wanted to hurt her, or Carter like I did, and because of me and my selfishness I lost the two most important people in my life.

"What the fuck are you doing here Ash, I thought Carter told yo ass to leave." Hearing somebody call my name stirred me out of my thoughts. I looked up from my grocery list and saw Davon standing near my basket holding Aubree's hand.

"Oh, um I'm living in the condo that daddy let me use."

"As in Pooh's pop?" I nodded my head yes and put my head down.

"Yo if she finds out that you been living there, she is going to flip the fuck out."

"Please don't tell them you saw me," I begged. He looked like he was contemplating which made me nervous.

"Man, I ain't gone say shit but you gone have to be more discreet, here take little mama and go home I get this shit and anything

else you need. Text me the address so I can drop this shit off," I nodded
the left with my daughter in my hand.

Present

Ever since that day the we bumped into each other in the
grocery store we have been inseparable,

"I'm coming Davon damn let me see if I have any mail then
we can leave with yo impatient ass," I walked in the dining room
and saw that I had mail scattered everywhere, but something
caught my eyes. I grabbed the paper that had dried up Henney
on it and read it.

"Oh my God he found out about the abortion," I whispered. I had a feeling that I am the reason why he ended up in a
car accident.

"What the fuck is wrong with you?" Davon said behind
me. I jumped and balled up the letter.

"Umm nothing I just notice that he opened my mail that's
all, I'm ready to go, we have to go pick up Bree from your
mother's house," I said changing the subject.

"Yea ah ight come on, we have to stop at the hospital
first," I nodded and followed him out of the house. If Pooh ever
finds out about this she might kill me.
• •

"Bro what the fuck is she doing here with you?" Killa said
as soon as we walked in the room.

"Don't worry about all that, what the fuck did you want
with me Devin?" Davon asked sounding irritated. Ever since the
argument that Pooh, and I had they really haven't been talking
and that I not normal for them.

"That don't even matter anymore, she needs to leave before Pooh comes out the bathroom," Killa said with fear in his eyes.

"She ain't going anywhere my nigga, Pooh needs to lear..."

"Davon don't even finish that sentence bro, Ash look sis I don't know what the fuck is going on with you and this idiot here, but I think you need to leave right now. I can't even protect you from what might happen if B saw you here" Killa said

"Bitch you got an abortion, and didn't tell me?" Before I could respond to Pooh, her ass jumped on me and started punching me with so much force I thought I was going to die.

"Bitch you're the reason why he is in here, I'm gone kill yo stupid ass," Killa was trying to hold her back but it wasn't working. The only thing that was able to stop her was the sound of Carter's Machine flat lining. The doctors rushed in and made all of us leave. When I looked at Pooh her Chocolate skin was now purple which scared me.

"Baby I need for you to breath okay," Killa said trying to get her to calm down. Her eyes rolled in the back of her head and she fell to the ground.

"OH MY GOD BIANCA!" I screamed and ran towards her.

"Somebody help my girl is not breathing," Killa said in a frantic tone.

"Please don't leave me bestfriend," I silently cried.

115

CHAPTER 19

Pooh

"**L**ord what the fuck happened," I said while try-ing to grabbing my head which felt like some-body kept stabbing me with a sharp ass knife. I don't remember what happened, all I remember is seeing my bestfriend flatlining, and the doctor's rushing in, but anything before or after that was a total blur. I looked in the corner and seen Devin in the chair knocked out.

"Devin, wake yo pretty ass up!" I yelled. His eyes popped opened he and mugged me causing me to laugh.

"Yo black ass wake up talking shit, are you okay?" He got out the chair and walked towards me, this man can make any-thing look sexy. He leaned down and kissed my lips which I gladly accepted.

"Yea I'm okay, what is this shit on me Dev?" I tried to lift my arms, but I Couldn't something was holding down. I was get-ting pissed off and Dev saw it.

"Aye calm yo ass down."

"Why the fuck am I strapped to a hospital bed Devin?"

"Yo crazy ass saw Ash and passed out cause you haven't ate and yo blood pressure was up, then when you woke up and you started acting like a fucking nut again so they had to restrain you," he explained looking mad as fuck. I busted out laughing

"Did I at least hit the bitch?" I asked unfazed about what he just said, that's when everything hit me. I went to Carter's house to get him some clothes, but I didn't even make it to his room cause I saw a piece of paper saying that she aborted my best friend's baby.

"That's not the point Bianca, yall need to talk," I ignored him cause I was looking at the plate that was sitting on his lap, and I didn't want to talk about it because me having a conversation with her is never going to happen.

"Did my daddy make that?" He nodded and unwrapped it.

"Yea and he already put sugar in it."

"AYE MY NIGGA!" My daddy know I love his spaghetti. Devin leaned over and put a spoonful in my mouth, and I moaned, his spaghetti is that good.

"Really B?"

"Hell yea! Have you ever had my Daddy's spaghetti?" I asked

"No"

"Niggaa, eat some?" He put a little on the fork and ate some. He looked at me and moaned. I started cracking up.

"Nigga did you just moan?" Kenyon said walking in the door with Rock, Kayin, and Kj behind him.

"Um can somebody please take this shit off of me?"

"Yea let me go get a doctor," Kj said.

"Nigga if you eat any more of my shit, I'm gone fuck you up," I said to Dev. As soon as the doctor took that shit off of me, I snatched my plate from Dev and started eating.

"You're not supposed to eat that, give it here." The doctor said while frowning and trying to grab my plate.

"You gone try to grab my plate after you just took this shit off my arms, do you really think that's a smart idea sir?"

"But you can't eat that."

"My wigga if you don't get yo pale ass out my sister face I'm gone beat yo ole Screech looking ass, ole Saved by the Bell ass nigga" Kenyon crazy ass said which caused us to burst out laughing.

"Can I go see my best friend?" I asked almost forgetting that he was in the hospital. Everybody looked at me with a sad expression on their face. I looked at Kj and he looked like he was about to cry, that along had me ready to go off because my brother rarely cries.

"What, can yall tell me what happened to Carter please?" I cried.

"Sis I'm sorry but.."

"NO NO NO NO, please tell me you're joking Kj." The way he looked at me broke my heart. I quickly got up snatched the wires off of me and ran out the room. I didn't give a fuck about anything but Carter at the moment.

"Why were you acting crazy out there Pooh?"

"Ahh!" I ran towards Carter crying, I hugged and kissed all over him. I can't believe that his ass is up and talking.

"Pooh that's enough I can't fucking breathe!" Carter said. Something clicked in my head and I slapped the fuck outta him, he grabbed his face and frowned.

"What the fuck Bianca!"

"Why would yo dumb ass try to kill yourself, and why would you tell those bitches out there to tell me you was dead?"

Because they told me that you showed yo ass out there, and you had to learn the hard way. Come on now best friend, you know me better than that, I didn't know I was taking all those pills I blacked out."

"I should beat yo ass!" He laughed

"Aye chill, you need to talk to Ash," when I saw that he was serious I wanted to put his ass back in a coma.

"She is the reason why you're in here Carter!" I yelled. I'm getting tired of everybody telling me that I need to talk to her.

"You heard what I said, now take yo fonky ass home yo ass smell sour," I kissed his cheek and left with Devin.

"Where are my kids Devin?" I asked

"At my mom's house with Bree"

"Can you go get them please?"

"Okay that's fine"

"Never mind, can we just go home, I just wanna shower and be under you." He smirked

"Who said I wanna be under yo ugly ass," He joked. I mushed his head and enjoyed the ride home. When we got to the house I went straight upstairs and got in the shower. I washed up and threw my hair in a ponytail, put on one of Devin's t-shirts and went to find my baby. He was in his office looking through paperwork.

"Come here," He demanded feeling my presence. I walked over to him and pressed my body against his. He kissed me deeply and pulled my hair which caused me to let out a soft moan. I tried to slide my hand in his basketball shorts, but he quickly stopped me.

"Nah ma come on, let's go watch tv." He pulled my hand and walked to the theater room. I went to pop some popcorn while he got a movie started. I sat in between his legs, and re-laxed. He stuffed a handful of popcorn in his mouth then played the movie.

"Have you talked to yo brother Daddy?" I asked.

"Nah, I'm not fucking with him."

"You need to talk to him baby, whatever Ash and I have going on don't have anything to do with y'all."

"Alright I will talk to him damn!" He was pissed but I really didn't care, ;ife was too short.

"Everybody is coming over here tomorrow just to chill is that coo with you?" He asked while kissing my lips.

"I guess its coo, just as long as I get some dick before every-body get here tomorrow," I said while grinding on his dick. He grabbed a handful of my hair and pulled my head towards him.

"Well what are you waiting on mama, do yo thang shorty." I quickly got up and stripped out of my clothes while he pulled his dick out of his shorts. Before he could change his mind, I quickly straddled his lap and eased down on his dick. The feeling of his penis pulsating inside of me, and him literally ripping me apart drove me crazy.

"Fuck mama, yo shit is fucking wet." He grunted while slamming his thick rod inside with every stroke. I bent down and kissed him passionately while bouncing on his dick.

"Shit daddy this shit feels soo good!" I screamed while trying to get out of his grip.

"Get yo ass up mama, I'm not done with you, this is what you wanted right?" He picked me up then bent me over across the chair. Without any warning he rammed his dick inside of me causing me to yell out in pain and pleasure.

"Baby wait, it's too much, I can't take it!" I tried to push him away, but he grabbed my arms and held them behind my back.

"Who pussy is this Bianca?"

"Fuck it's your baby it's all yours, I'm about to cum daddy shit!"

"I'm right behind you mama, cum all on this dick." He reached forwards and started playing with my clit. Within a couple of seconds, I was Cumming all over his dick.

"Fuck baby here it comes," he moaned in my ear while spilling his seeds deep inside of me. We both collapsed on the chair breathing heavy.

"You want some Juice?" He asked me while getting comfortable in the seat.

"Nigga go to sleep with yo crazy ass," I kissed his lips and laid on his chest.

• •

"Pooh stop fucking cheating," Kj yelled while getting

frustrated. We were currently playing 2k, and I was beating his ass.

"Nigga I ain't cheating, you just can't play."

"Fuck you," He cursed. I busted out laughing, his ass was so fucking mad.

"Kj you must be getting yo ass whopped in here," Carter said while walking in the house.

"Shut the fuck up bitch, wassup baby" Kj said. Staci walked over to Kj and kissed him. I looked between Carter and Kj confused on how she got here. As soon as I woke up this morning Kj called me and told me that Carter was raising hell at the hospital because they wasn't trying to discharge him, the next thing I know his yellow ass is limping in my house with a big ass smirk on his face.

"Ummm how the fuck did she get here?' Staci looked at me then smirked

"I rode with my best friend." This bitch said being petty, not knowing that she was about to get her ass whopped.

"Bitch didn't I tell you to stay away from Carter?" I said as I got up and stood in front of her. Kj stood in between us and pushed me back.

"Move Kj so I can beat this bitch ass." Staci said which caused me to burst out laughing

"Sis please" Kj begged while looking at me.

"I ain't gone touch that bitch Kj" I shot back.

"I think her, and Carter are fucking on the low." She tried to whisper. I turned around and punched that bitch dead in her mouth.

"You got one more time to disrespect me, and I'm gone beat your ass. Bring yo ass upstairs so I can talk to you cause you are starting to piss me the fuck off."

"Ah hell nah, Staci if you go up those stairs, you're dumb as fuck," Kayin said

"Dead bitch walking!" We all busted out laughing at Kenyon's stupid ass.

"Shut up Kenyon, bitch get yo stupid ass up, I ain't hit you that hard."

"Shiiitt, you got my mouth hurting," Kenyon said while holding his mouth.

"Kenyon please shut the fuck up, bting yo ass on before I drag you up here," I yelled while looking at her, She slowly got up and walked up the stairs.

"If heaven was a mile away!"

"Would I pack up my bags and leave this world behind," I cracked up laughing at Davon and Kenyon.

"Davon and Kenyon please get out of my house." When I made it up the stairs to my room, I closed the door and stood in front of Staci.

"I didn't come up here to beat yo ass, I just want you to know that I don't play about Carter. Carter and I have been bestfriend for a long ass time and not once have we fucked or anything. Carter has been there for me since I could remember, it's always been Kj, Carter, and I, I'm willing to share my brother because he gets on my nerves sometimes but when it comes to Carter that is a huge NO, I would beat somebody's ass for him.

We have been glued to the hip and I refuse to give him away, I'm very territorial when it comes to him." I explained, meaning every word that was coming out my mouth.

"You said you don't share but Ash and Carter were dating." She responded sounding confused.

"First of all, its Ashton to you, and that's different, Ash and I were best friends, so I didn't care cause most of the time I'm with one of them."

"Aw okay, I understand I didn't know you were that close; I will fall back."

"Bitch you really didn't have a choice, oh and with my brother, I don't play about him, if you hurt him, I will kill you."

"So, are we coo, cause I could really use a friend"

"Yea we're coo just stay away from Carter, but we good boo" I tried to hug her, but she flinched.

"Girl I ain't gone hit you" I laughed.

"Good cause you hit like a nigga," We laughed and walked downstairs, everybody just sat around and looked at us.

"Sis are yall coo?" Kj said with a raised eyebrow.

"Yea nigga we good, she's still breathing ain't she?" I said while walking over to Devin and sitting on his lap. I leaned back and kissed his soft lips he was sitting there looking all good, he was dressed down in some Nike sweats, a white t-shirt, and some slides.

"You better stop looking at me like that for I take yo ass upstairs," he whispered in my ear and reached forward grabbing my breast.

"Aye stop that shit!" Kayin said, Kenyon's ass was acting like he was about to throw up, when ass of a sudden there was a knock on the door which caused us to automatically stop talking.

"I'll go get the door, stay right here." Dev said I nodded and got up so he could go and get and get the door.

"Can you please go upstairs and get my nephews; I don't know why you keep those niggas isolated from everybody anyways." Kj said fussing like he always do.

"I'll go get them with yo cry baby ass." I went upstairs to get my handsome babies who were soundly asleep.

"Come on my babies, Uncle Kj acts like he can't let yall sleep in peace," I kissed their chubby cheeks and made my way downstairs. I stooped mid step when I saw Ash walking into my living room.

"Auntie Ash I missed you soo much!" Vonna said while running towards her and hugged her tightly, if I didn't have my babies in my hand, I would've beat her ass.

"Why is she here Devin?"

"Baby I didn't tell her to come, she came here by herself, don't do anything stupid in front of our kids though," He said while walking towards me and taking the babies.

"Ashton why are you here?" I asked getting straight to the point.

"I want to work things out between us Pooh, I really miss our friendship." I looked at her contemplating on what to do. Apart of me wanted to forgive her because I miss my sister, but a part of me wanted to beat the dog shit out of her for everything she did to me and Carter.

"Come on let's go outside and talk, and Devin talk to your brother." I said while looking at him. He just ignored me and continued to play with the twins, I just hope that I am able to keep my cool while talking to her.

"So what's going on, why did you want to talk to me?" I asked while sitting down on the bench.

"I just wanted to apologize for everything that I put you and Carter through, I really do want you to know that it was not my intention to hurt you when I was messing with Ahmad," She said in one breath.

"Then what was your intentions Ash, you didn't stop to think that your action was going to hurt me, what would make you do such a thing to me? You are more than a best friend, you are my fucking sister, so for you to do something like that to me hurt me, then you bring yo loose pussy ass to the hospital with Davon and say all of those hurtful things to me. Ash what is going on, why didn't you tell me about you and Ahmad, or that fact that you got an abortion?" I asked while wiping the tears that were falling, I couldn't even look at her without crying.

"I wasn't thinking at the time Bianca you have to believe me; all I could think about was the fact that he acted like he liked me. I wasn't thinking about you or how this would make you feel at the time, I was being selfish, and I regret that deeply. All of the things that I did was about me looking for love in all of the wrong places, I am so sorry Bianca I truly am, and if you can find it in your heart to forgive me I promise I will not hurt you anymore. I will be nothing but honest and truthful with you, the reason why I didn't tell you about the abortion is because I knew that you were going to take up for Carter."

"That's not true Ashton and you know it, Carter may be my best friend, but I am still a woman at the end of the day, I would've been mad, but at the same time I would have understood Ash. You know what let's just start over, I'm never going to forget what you did, but I am willing to forgive, you just have to promise me that you are going to keep it real with me."

"I promise I will, no more lies or secrets." She looked me in my eyes when she said it. I just smiled and hugged her, I'm glad that I have my sister back in my life, I just hope she doesn't make me regret it.

CHAPTER 20

Killa

I was mad as fuck when my alarm went off this morning. Once B and Ash came back in and told everybody that they were coo again we all turned up all night and now I'm tired as fuck, but I had to get up and go to the shop, I haven't been up there in a while. I looked down at my baby, and like always she was under me sleep. I kissed her lips and got out of the bed, even when she's sleep, she is the most beautiful girl I ever met. I went to the bathroom to handle my hygiene, and threw on some joggers, a Nike shirt, and my slides.

"Baby I'm about to go give me a kiss," I said while kissing her cheek, but she started that whining shit that she know I hate.

"Devin please leave me alone, I'll call you later." She pulled the covers over her head but I snatched them back off.

"Stop fucking playing with me Bianca, you know I hate that shit!" I got on top of her and just started kissing her all over her face.

"Devin stop please, you're being so irritating this morning" I busted out laughing at her dramatic ass, her ass was really sitting here crying.

"Stop fucking crying, call me when you get up," I kissed her one last time then left. By the time I made it to the shop, it was cars everywhere.

"Damn it's packed as fuck in here, what's up yall." I greeted while walking in the door.

"Hey boss what's going on?" Toy ass said while eating a big ass burger being unprofessional as fuck. Her ass better be lucky she is my sis.

"Aye Killa can you hook me up?" One of my clients asked.

"Yea man come sit down"

"Where you been man, I been here every day for like two months looking for you."

"Man, I've been busy, but I'm back now," I can already tell today is going to be a long day.
. . . .

I've been cutting hair all day and a nigga is tired. Just as I was about to start cutting again, I looked down at my phone and my wife was calling me.

"Hold on man let me take this call, what's up mama?" I answered.

"Hey baby, have you ate?"

"No, I been cutting hair all day."

"Vonna and I wanna take you out for lunch."

"Hey daddy!" Vonna screamed through the phone which made me smile.

"Hey princess, thats fine baby come up here and we can go get something to eat."

"Okay baby, Im on my way"

"Love you mama"

"I love you too daddy," I hung up and Toy was looking directly at me.

"What Toy?"

"Look at you all in love and shit, got yo little hoes over there mad," I looked over towards where she was pointing, and it was a bunch of hoes mugging me.

"Shut yo crazy ass up Toy," she just laughed and continued to eat like she didn't have clients waiting on her. Thirty mins later my two favorite girls walked in dressed alike, they had on some jeans a white V-Neck and some Sandals.

"Daddy!" Vonna said while running toward me and waiting for me to pick her up.

"Come here Vonna, wait until daddy gets done cutting hair," B said while blowing me a kiss. Vonna ran toward B and sat on her lap.

"So yo happy ass just come in here and act like you don't see nobody," Toy said to B

"Girl ain't nobody worried about you, aren't you supposed to be doing hair anyways?"

"Bitch don't worry about me, that's what I'm about to do now."

"Auntie Toy can I help you?" Vonna asked.

"Yea come on baby cakes," Vonna got down and ran towards Toy. I knew it was about to be some shit when this bitch who I used to let suck my dick walked in with her friends.

"Hey Killa, can you hook me up," she winked, then licked her lips.

"Ask Toy I'm about to go to lunch." I said shooting her down.

"I'll just wait on you to get back," she walked away and sat by B who wasn't paying her any attention.

"Girl he is still fine; I just want to fuck him right here."

"Bitch you better be quiet. I heard he got a girlfriend now; she might be in here."

"Bitch all of these hoes in here are either ugly or fat, and Toy is his sister, so shut up," B just shook her head and laughed, she got up and walked toward me.

"Baby I'm going to be in the car waiting, I don't wanna show my ass in here," I grabbed her by the waist and kissed her passionately, I had to let her fine ass go cause I ready to bend her ass over in front of everybody in here. She grabbed her purse and walked out.

"Look at you showing affection in a place of business," Toy said.

"So that's what you like now Killa, fat ugly bitches?" Krystal said.

"Bitch if you don't shut yo Tony the Tiger built ass up, he obviously didn't want you." I busted out laughing at Toy. When you make her mad there is no telling what will come out of her mouth.

"So you just gone let her talk to me like that Devin?"

"The only reason why I haven't said anything is because my daughter is in here, but you and yo broke ass friends can get the fuck out my shit."

"Yea get out my daddy's shop ugly!" Vonna yelled

"Vonna watch yo mouth and get over here," B said causing me to look towards the door.

"I thought you was in the car."

"You were taking too long."

"Well I'm done now, aye my dude this shit on the house, I'm sorry for all of the interruption," he paid me anyways and walked out.

"Toy watch my shit I will be back, and don't touch nothing either," I fussed.

"Nigga if you don't get yo yellow ass out of here and take the Ninja Turtles with you," We all busted out laughing. I looked at Krystal who looked mad as fuck.

• •

"Do you gotta go back to work?" B whined.

"Yea but come in and keep me company, Toy ass is leaving early."

"Okay I'm gone drop Chunks off and I'll come back," I looked in the back seat and my baby was knocked out. We ended up at Chuck E Cheese, and she played herself to sleep.

"Alright text me when you're on your way back," I leaned over and kissed her lips.

"Nigga what type of lunch was that?" Toy asked as soon as I walked in.

"A boss lunch, what time are you leaving?"

"Never bitch, you're stuck with me, plus my bitch as date canceled on me," I laughed and sat in my chair.

"Just the nigga I wanted to see, line me up real quick," Kj said while walking in with Davon behind him.

"I got you," Kj sat in my chair and I got to work.

"Um nigga you don't speak," Toy said mugging Kj.

"My bad what's up Kenyon. I mean Toy," Kj smirked. Kenyon and Toy act like they couldn't stand each other, but we all knew the truth, both of their crazy asses was feeling each other, but was too stubborn to admit it.

"What's up yall" Ash said while walking in with Staci behind her.

"Well damn, its a party in Twin Cuts today!" Toy said.

"Toy can you hook me up I need a sew in" Ash asked.

"Yea baby come sit down, aye if yo nigga ain't hitting right call me." Toy whispered in Ash ear fucking with Davon

"Toy make me beat yo ass," Davon said. We all started laughing nut stopped when we noticed that B was standing at the door with a frown on her face.

"You're really fucking with Davon huh?" B said looking at Ash

"Pooh don't start," Kj said. B mugged everybody and went into my office.

"I'll go talk to her" Ash said.

"Are you tryna get yo ass beat, you dumb as fuck if you go in there." Kj said.

"Just come sit down baby, her ass ain't worth it." Davon looked at me and sat down. I laughed then shook my head.

" You better watch what the fuck you say about my bitch nigga, Kj I'll be back bro" He nodded and continued to talk to Staci.

"Bae what's going on, talk to daddy," she was sitting on my desk texting. I stood in between her legs and pulled her jeans off, when I started messaging her clit and her head fell back, and she started moaning.

"Talk to me baby, what's wrong?"

"Fuck Devin," I pulled my fingers out and unbuckled my pants.

"Get up and turn around," She got up and leaned on the desk. I slid inside of her and started thrusting in and out of her warm pussy.

"Oh, my Shit fuck Devin" she tried to run but I pulled her hair towards me.

"Stop running ma, take that shit" I started giving her long deep strokes which caused her to start shaking.

"Im finna cum!"

"Cum with me baby," I leaned forward and started playing with her clit.

"Fuck baby shit!" I grunted and released my seeds inside of her. I grabbed her hand and went to the bathroom.

"Eventually you are going to have to talk to Ash and hear each other out, You're still mad at her for what she did to Carter, but you are going to have to let that go baby," she rolled her eyes and cleaned my dick off.

"I'm not talking to her Dev, let it go." I just walked away and sat in the chair. She walked out the bathroom and straddled my lap.

"Baby I know you're mad, but you have to understand where I'm coming from. You're telling me to talk to her, but have you talked to your brother?" When she asked me that I just looked at her.

"My point exactly, at least me and Ash came to an understanding last night, now get up and go finish my brother's hair," I hate when her funny looking ass was right, that's my baby though. She kissed me one last time and got up so she can walk out the door. When she was on her feet her phone fell out her pocket and lit up.

"Who the fucking is texting you from an unknown number Bianca?" I fussed while looking at her phone.

"I don't know, they have been texting me for a while now," She shrugged, I grabbed her phone and opened the message.

678-555-2377: Watch yo back lil mama, I would hate for your kids to grow up motherless.

"Yo what the fuck is this shit Bianca, you been getting these messages and haven't said anything to anybody?" I yelled in her face, she frowned and pushed me back.

"Nigga first of all I didn't think it was a big deal, I thought it was just one of yall playing on my phone.

"We are getting you a new phone, and a new number come on," I grabbed her hand and dragged her out the office.

"The next time yall nasty asses want to fuck make sure you let us know, but I could tell you was murdering that cat, I taught you well bro." Toy said while laughing, normally I would talk shit right back, but I'm not in the mood for that. I had to find out who is playing on my wife's phone. Davon stopped cutting Kj's hair and notice something was wrong with me. No matter what's going on between me and my brother, he could always tell when something is wrong with me.

"Bro you good?" He asked looking concerned.

"Nah, when you get done with Kj's head I need to speak with all yall. Toy close the shop down, and we will be closed until further notice," she nodded and started getting ready to close.

"Bro what the fuck is going on, you never close the shop down." Kayin said.

"I'll tell yall in a minute, just call Carter and tell him to meet us at Unc's house," without any further questions he started making the calls.

"Baby don't you think you're being a little dramatic?" B said while walking towards me. It amazes me how smart this girl is, but how naive she can be at the same time.

"I need you to get the fuck out my face right now Bianca, because the way Im feeling about you right now is not a good feeling." She rolled her eyes then walked away. Once the shop was closed down, we all got in our cars and made out way towards Unc house.

"What's so important that you had to drag me and D out the bed." Unc said while rolling up a blunt.

"So apparently somebody has been texting your daughters' phone from an unknown number, threating all of us." I said getting straight to the point.

"What the fuck you mean texting her, how long has this been going on?" Kj asked.

"Nigga just what the fuck I said, when we were in my office her phone fell out her jeans, when pick it up I notice a text from an unknown number. I asked her who it is, and she basically said that she thought it was one of us playing on her phone, she said that is has been on for a while now, but she never really paid any attention to it." I explained.

"Yo daughter has got to be the dumbest person that I have ever met," Kenyon said while shaking his head.

"Watch yo mouth about my daughter son, Killa do you still have her phone?"

"No but I have the number."

"Okay give me the number, and I'll have my man track it down. Now what I'm about to say I don't want any of yall being offended, but I think it's time that we come out of retirement." My pops while looking at Unc.

"I don't think that's a good idea pops, think about it, as soon as whoever this God person is finds out that yall are out of retirement all hell is going to break loose. I think yall should just stay in the background for right now," Kj said.

"Now son, I have been calm and understanding about this situation for too long, when they put my baby girl in the middle of this, that's where I draw the line. Now I'm gone say this only once so yall better be listening. We want all of the information that you have on this God person. Me and D are going to track this number and see who is behind it, then we will come up with a plan as a team, do I make myself clear?" He looked at each and every one of us making sure that we understood what he was saying.

"Yea pops we got you, but what are we gone do about that girls, and the kids?" Kayin asked.

"They are going to go to a hotel under a different name just to keep them safe," We all nodded.

"Kj go tell yo sister to come down here real quick, everybody get out except for Devin," Unc said looking directly at me.

"If you do anything to me soon, I will kill you." My pops said then walked out.

"What's going on daddy?" Bianca said walking in and sitting on his lap like a little kid. He kissed her cheek then focused on me.

"So, what are your intentions with my daughter?" He asked getting straight to the point.

"I'm going to be honest, when I first met B I wasn't feeling her, I didn't like the fact that she had all of yall wrapped around her finger, but when we started getting to know each other, I found out that she was a sweet person. She is good with my OUR kids, she is honest, loyal, respectful, sweet, down to earth, and beautiful. Since we met, I've been changing for the better. She always keep me laughing, calm, and in line, I want to marry B, and start a family with her. I want to be the reason she is happy and be the man she deserves," I said then looked at B who was crying her eyes out.

"My daughter has been through so much in her life. She has been let down, hurt, and betrayed. I love all my children to death but Pooh and I have a special bond. Please don't hurt my baby, treat her with respect, do you love my daughter?" I looked at B and she had her head down, which she knew I hated. I grabbed her chin and kissed her lips.

"I do love her."

"You see those tears, she will never admit it, but she is scared to love, don't make me have to kill you because you hurt my daughter," he got up, kissed her face then left. She wiped her tears and sat on my lap.

"You are so cute when you're being romantic," she said while pinching my cheeks.

"You like that romantic shit huh?" I smirked. She blushed and nodded her head.

"Well come on and let me put a baby in you."

"Why do you have to mess up the moment? Soooooo you know my birthday is coming up right," she said sounding like a little girl.

"What does that have to do with anything Bianca?"

"What are you getting me negro?"

"I ain't getting yo spoiled ass sh.." I stopped talking when I heard arguing coming from the living room.

"That sounds like Ash and Carter arguing," I said. B jumped up off my lap and ran to the living room.

"We haven't even been broken up that long and yo hoe ass already on to the next nigga!" Carter yelled from behind Kj and Kayin who was trying to hold him back. I just laughed and sat down. I told my brother that Carter was not going to take this too well.

"Watch yo mouth when you're talking to her my nigga." Davon said.

"Nigga fuck you, yo bitch just had my dick down her throat a couple of weeks ago, but know she's yo girl, fuck outta here with that pussy shit Davon."

"Carter please calm down so we can discuss this like adults." B said trying to calm him down but obviously it wasn't working.

"You know what fuck all yall bitches, best friend it's nothing against you, but yo family is on some snake shit." He kissed her cheek then walked away. I just sat back and laughed.

"What the fuck are you laughing for, you're supposed to be my bro, but you didn't have my back." Davon said sounding like a bitch.

"Nigga you sound like a straight bitch right now, I told you the first time that you don't need to fuck with her because she's nothing but trouble, but did you listen to me?" I shot back while walking towards him.

"Baby please don't start let's just go home okay, daddy can yo grandkids stay here?" B said

"You know they can." She smile and walked over towards me.

"Baby please let's just go." She begged, I looked down at her and just walked out the door, my brother is going to learn to listen to me.

CHAPTER 21

Pooh

One Month Later

I t's my twenty fourth birthday and I wasn't in the mood to celebrate. It's been a month since I heard from Carter, and he's talking to everybody but me. Ash acts like she is over it, and it is not her fault, but we all know that she is not.

"Happy Birthday mommy!" Vonna said while jumping on the bed.

"Happy Birthday mama!" Dev got his big ass on the bed and started jumping.

"Yall are so crazy!" I laughed. Dev picked up Vonna sat on the bed.

"Get up, my mama will be here to get Vonna in a minute." Dev said while kissing my lips.

"Well move so I can take a shower," I flipped the covers back and went in the bathroom so I could take a shower. Once I was done, I slipped on one of Devin's t'shirt and a pair of pants, so I could go downstairs.

"Granny I wanna stay with mommy and daddy," Vonna whined. I hated when my baby cried.

"Come here Chunks," she hopped off the couch and walked over to me.

"Go with Granny tonight, and we can get our hair, nails, and feet done tomorrow."

"Shopping to?" She pouted.

"Of course, baby."

"Hell no, yall just did all that shit last week," Dev said. Vonna ignored his comment gave me a hug and kiss and ran to her daddy.

"Bye grumpy pants," she kissed him and ran out the door. I sat on the couch and Dev scooted back so he was leaning in between my legs.

"What do you want to do for your birthday," he asked never taking his eyes off of the game.

"I don't know I guess we can go out to eat or something, I really don't want to do anything, and my best friend is not here."

"Alright I'll hook it up for you," I tilted his head back and kissed his lips. He turned off the game so we could go upstairs and get back in bed, but he got in the shower instead.

"Happy Birthday sis!" Davon said while walking in with a big ass Teddy Bear, and like ten balloons. As soon as that situation happened with him and Carter, I forced Dev to make up with his brother.

"You are so dramatic, but thank you"

"Let me holla at you about something," Davon said sounding serious.

"Nigga get the fuck out" Dev yelled from the shower.

"Nigga shut the fuck up, text me pooh," Davon said then walked out. As soon as he stepped out the shower I almost passed out, his dick was just lying on his thigh chilling. I have been extremely horny lately and the way he was looking had me wanting to take advantage of him.

"Is this what you want mama?" He dropped his towel and grabbed his dick. I nodded my head and he laughed.

"To bad you have to wait until tonight," He said then

walked back in the bathroom, I was so mad I started crying.

"I know yo ass ain't sitting there crying." When I didn't say anything, he burst out laughing.

"Get yo horny ass up and get dress, we were supposed to meet the family an hour ago," I got up, took a shower and put on some shorts, a pink shirt that said "Birthday Girl", and some nude heels.

"I'm going to let you wear that cause it's your birthday, but don't get fucked up, and fix yo fucking attitude," Dev said then smacked my ass. I just rolled my eyes then walked away, I was real life mad at his ass for not giving me what I wanted.

• •

"Are you still mad at me ma?" Dev asked while pouting. We were sitting outside of IHOP cause Kenyon's crazy ass got us put out.

"No, I'm not," I admitted with a smile on my face. He kissed me and wrapped his arms around my waist.

"What time are we supposed to be going to dinner?"

"Yo killa we gotta roll now!" Davon said while heading to the car. I looked between the both of them trying to figure out if they were being serious or not.

"I'm so sorry baby," He tried to kiss me, but I quickly moved my head.

"Nigga now!" Kj yelled trying to get his attention.

"Watch out," I moved out his way so he could leave, I watched him as he got in the car then drove off.

"Come on bitch, let's go get our nails done," Ash suggested.

"No, I just wanna go home and watch Netflix," not giving her a chance to respond I got in my Car and left.

Ash: Meet me at my house at 8:45 and wear Red. If you don't come, I will drag yo ass out of the house.

Me: Okay damn, I'll be there

I knew her ass wasn't gone let me chill for the night.

• •

"Okay bitch I see you!" Staci said while opening the door, I had on a Red skintight dress, black red bottoms, black lipsticks, and a black choker.

"Aye, that's my best friend that's my bestfriend!" Ash crazy ass jumped on her car and started twerking, so of course my ass started twerking too.

"AYE, FUCK IT UP, FUCK IT UP!" Staci and Ash was hyping me up. I didn't give a fuck tonight. It was my birthday and I was about to fuck some shit up. My phone started ringing and it was Dev irritating ass.

"Yes Devin."

"Take that shit off now!" He yelled

"Nope" I said then hung up. I wasn't gone see him tonight so he couldn't control what I wear.

"Come on bitches lets go," I yelled. We got in Ash's Car and left, and when we pulled up to our destination, I was mad as fuck when I noticed that we were at Paradise.

"Why are we here?"

"Bitch what you mean, fuck those niggas, they left us to fucking work, so we are about to run up a tab on the fucking house!" Staci ratchet ass said. We all got out of the car and headed towards the door, as soon as we made it in the was a banner that said Happy Birthday on it.

"Listen listen, the Birthday girl just arrived, everybody let's give it up for Bianca one time!" The dj yelled. Everybody yelled surprised and my cry baby ass started crying. I looked in the VIP area and my whole family was there; I ran up the stairs and hugged everybody.

"Thank you so much Kj," I cried while hugging him.

"Don't thank me sis, this was all Killa's idea," I turned around and looked at him and he was mugging the fuck outta me.

"Thank you daddy," I tried to kiss him but he mushed me in my face.

"I told you to take that shit off."

"But it's my birthday, and you're over here looking like a snack and shit, I had to match yo fly," he smirked then took his hat off making me want to take advantage of him. Who told my nigga to go out and get a fresh cut?

"Damn bitch can we share," Staci ass said.

"Shut the fuck up Staci," Kj roared causing all of us to laugh.

"ISSA SNACK!" Everybody busted out laughing at Kenyon's irritating ass. Devin ran his tongue across his bottom lip, and that's when I noticed he had his bottom grill in.

"Damn daddy, you gone make me take you home tonight and do something strange for a piece of change," I whispered causing him to laugh.

"Shut yo silly ass up and turn around," I turned around and saw Carter walking up the stairs. I started jumping up and down and crying.

"I told you not to wear that little ass shit!" Devin yelled as he tried to pull my dress down. I ignored him, ran and jumped in my best friends' arms.

"OH MY GOD CARTER!!!!!"

"Happy birthday baby girl," he whispered whisper then kissed my cheek.

"Um excuse me," I look behind him and Tiffany was standing there looking ugly. Tiffany was Carter's ex-girlfriend, who broke up with him because she said she needed somebody who could afford her. He know that I hate that bitch, so I don't even know why her brought her.

"Pooh, Tiffany and I are dating." Carter explained.

"Nope not tonight, Tiffany yo snake ass gotta go, Carter I love you but this makes you look real suspect my nigga." I walked away and saw this bitch sitting on Dev's lap. He was trying to push her off, but she wasn't moving. I walked over there and calmly pushed her out my nigga's lap, and just looked at her debating on if I wanted to beat her ass, but my attention went elsewhere when I looked at Ash and saw her sitting on Davon's lap like she didn't have a care in the world.

"You see that babe?" I asked Dev while sitting on his lap.

"Mind yo business Bianca," he whispered in my ear. As soon as I heard Wild thoughts coming out the speaker, I started grinding on Devin's lap. When this song comes on everybody know that I'm about to show the fuck out.

"Yass bitch fuck it up!" My girls was hyping me up in the

background and that only made me go harder.

"Pooh stop that nasty shit!" Kj yelled

"Nigga stop looking, why did yo ass wear that dress when I told you not to?" Dev whispered while rubbing on my thigh.

"Pooh come get in our picture." Ash said interrupting us. After taking a few pictures with my girls, I turned around and Dev was sitting in the corner by his self looking good as fuck. I slowly walked over to him and straddled his lap.

"Why are you over here by yourself?" I asked.

"You never answered my question mama."

""What?"

"Why do you have on that short ass dress?"

"Ash told me to wear red and I haven't worn this before." I replied.

"You got panties on?" I smirked and nodded my head yes. his hand went up my dress and slid his fingers inside of me.

"Why did you lie B?"

"Fuck Devin," I moaned ignoring his question.

"Why are you so wet, get up really quick, I gotta feel you," when I got up he unbuckled his pants and freed his dick. With no hesitation, I straddled his lap and ease down on his dick but stopped because it was too much dick for me.

"Don't stop, take all of that shit ma," he pushed inside of me and we both froze.

"Fuck Devin," I started bouncing up and down on his dick

while he played with my clit.

"Fuck B yo pussy so wet," I bent down and put my face in his neck so I wouldn't scream.

"Oh my God daddy I'm about to cum!" He started going deeper making sure he hit my spot. All of a sudden, we both started moaning loudly as we reached our peak.

"Come on," he demanded as he slapped my ass and helped me up. When we walked in Kj's office we automatically went to the bathroom. I wrapped my arms around his neck and kissed his lips.

"If you ever give my shit away, I will kill you, do you understand me?" He said while kissing my neck.

"I'm always going to be yours daddy, come on lets go home so I can get some more dick," I whispered in his ear.

"Nah not yet I got one more gift for you come on mama," he grabbed my hand and dragged me out of the office and on to the stage.

"Dev what the fuck are you up to?" I asked giving him the side eyes, he just smirked and grabbed the mic from the Dj.

"I want to thank everybody for coming out to celebrate my baby's twenty fourth birthday, I can truly say that this was a success. Baby I want you to know that I love you so much, ever since I saw yo nappy headed ass I knew that I had to have you. You don't understand the impact you had on my life, and I appreciate you for that. We have our own family and I wouldn't trade that in for anything, you are like a breath of fresh air, and it would be a blessing if you would marry me," he gave the Dj the mic back and got down on one knee. When he opened the box, I saw the biggest ring ever, not being able to hold back the tears I burst out crying and just nodded my head. He had a big ass smile on my face as he slid the ring on my finger. I wrapped my arms around his and kissed him with so much passion.

"I love you so much Mrs. Lowe."

"I love you more Mr. Lowe," I responded while wiping the tear that was falling from his face, this was the best birthday I have ever had.

CHAPTER 22

Kj

"**B**aby wake up, yo daddy is calling you," Staci yelled while nudging me. I reached over and grabbed my phone from her.

"What's up pops?"

"Nothing much, do you think you can come by here before everybody else gets here?" He asked sounding serious. Today my pops is having our annual BBQ for the first day of summer.

"Yea I can, but what's going on pops, is everything okay?"

"Yea son everything is fine I just need to speak with you about something," the tone in his voice sounded urgent which made me worry.

"I'll be over there in about an hour or so, I have yo daughter's kids so it's gone take a while."

"Alright son well I will be here."

"Pops are you sure everything is okay?"

"I'm positive, I just need to talk to you so you can put your guns up killer."

"Yea ah ight," I said then hung up. What it was that my pops had to talk about was clearly bothering him, I just hope that it didn't piss me off.

"What was that all about?" Staci nosey ass asked.

"Why the fuck are you so nosey shorty, I can't get no privacy?" I asked playfully

"Nigga when yo little dick ass asked me to move in with you, privacy went out the window."

"Aye stop fucking playing with me, you know ain't nothing little about this thing right here," I grabbed my dicked and waved it around which caused her to lick her lips. Ever since we went out on our date we have been glued to the hip. Staci may have a few screws loose in here, but she is the girl that I have always wanted.

"You better put that thing up before yo nosey ass niece come bursting in the room like she always do," when she said that I quickly stuffed my dick back inside of my boxers. She was right about one thing; my niece was nosey just like her black ass mama.

"Are the twins up?"

"Amir is but you know, all Ashad do is sleep why?"

"Can you get the kids ready; we have to go to my pops house a little early."

"Yea baby that's no problem, do you know what he wants to talk to you about?"

"Nope, but we are about to find out," I kissed her lips then got out of bed to take a shower.

· ·

"What's up beautiful," I said while walking in the kitchen and kissing my mom on the cheek.

"Hey handsome what are you doing here this early?"

"You husband wanted to talk to me about something."

"NANA!" Vonna screamed while running in the kitchen. Even though my mama does not get along with Pooh, she still treat the kids like they were her grandchildren.

"Hey Nana's baby what's going on?"

"Can I help you cook Nana?"

"Yea you can go in the bathroom and wash your hands, where are my grandsons Kj?"

"In there with Staci," I said then walked away to the basement to find pops."

"What's going on old man?" I sat down next to my pops who was smoking a blunt while watching the news. Now I knew for a fact that something was bothering him because he never watch the new except for when something is heavy on his mind.

"Oh shit, what's going on pops?" He put the blunt out and just looked at me.

"Pops you good man, is Ma good?" I asked staring to get worried.

"I'm Bianca's father," He blurted out, which caused me to look at him weird.

"Pops what the fuck are you talking about, I already know that you're her father."

"No, I mean her biological father," once he said that I had to do a double take, did this man just say what I think he said.

"Pops what the fuck are you talking about, Uncle Tyrone is Pooh's biological father."

"Tyrone is Bianca's adopted father son," He admitted. I quickly stood up and just looked at him. I can't believe the words that are coming out of his mouth.

"Pops come on man; tell me you're just fucking with me."

"I can't tell you that son, I'm telling the truth."

"Wait so you was fucking Auntie Freeda behind Unc's and Mama's back?"

"Yes."

"And that's why ma hate Pooh because, you're biological daughter," he just looked at me with guilt in his eyes. I didn't even know what to say at this point, the fact that he has been lying to us this whole time is crazy, I can't even look at him the same.

"Pops this shit is fucked up, do uncle D know?"

"Yea he knows, I don't know what to do son."

"You need to tell her Pops, I understand that this might, nah fuck that, this is going to fuck up your relationship that you have with Bianca but you have to tell her, she has a right to know."

"I have a right to know what?" We both turned around so fast that I'm surprise we didn't break our neck. Pooh was standing at the bottom of the stairs with Amir bad ass on her hip.

"That I can't stop thinking about the shit that Ahmad did," I said quickly thinking of a lie.

"Well you gone have to get over it Kj, hey daddy." She walked over to my daddy and kissed his cheek. I just looked at my pops and shook my head. Once Pooh finds out about this shit, all hell gone break loose.

• •

"Baby what's wrong?" Staci said while fixing my plate. Ever since my pops told me that bullshit, I have been quiet.

"Nothing baby."

"Stop lying to me Ka'Mari," I looked at my sister and

looked back at Staci contemplating on what to do next.

"Pops is Pooh's biological father," I blurted out, she stopped fixing my plate and looked at me.

"Go tell her now."

"But."

"I don't care Ka'Mari you told her you would not keep anything else from her, tell her now, Pooh come here baby," Staci yelled in my ear, Pooh stopped talking to Carter and walked over towards us.

"What yall niggas want?" Pooh said while stealing a wing off of my plate.

"Come in the house, I need to tell you something," I whispered in her ear.

"Is it bad?" She asked sounding worried.

"Depends on how you take it, come on," we walked in the living room and sat down.

"What's up bro, are you okay?" Pooh asked as soon as we got comfortable, I just closed my eyes and blurted it out.

"Bianca, pops is your biological father," she looked at me for a minute then burst out laughing, she stopped laughing when she realized I wasn't.

"Wait are you serious Kj?" She asked above a whisper.

"Yes, I wanted to tell you, but I didn't know how you would feel," our father said while walking in, he tried to touch her, but she quickly snatched away.

"Did you know Kj," she asked crying, while looking at me

with sad eyes.

"I just found out today," she nodded then got up.

"I'm done with this family, every time I turn around its nothing but drama, fucking drama," she walked over to me and kissed me on my cheek.

"I'm sorry that you, Kayin, and Kenyon have to be in the middle of this, but I'm washing my hands with this family, I love you brother," she looked at me and walked away.

"What the fuck happened to my fucking sister?" Kayin stormed in with Kenyon behind him.

"She is just overreacting," my pops said while sitting down which instantly pissed me off.

"Overreacting, she just found out that you are her biological father. All her life she has been getting lied to, get the fuck outta here with that shit pops."

"What the fuck you mean biological father, pops what the fuck is going on?" Kenyon yelled.

"I'll leave you to discuss this with your kids, I'm gone," I said before walking out the door. I had to get out of there before I have to do something that I will regret.
. . . .

"Have you talked to my sister?" Kenyon asked while sitting across from me.

"Nah man, it's been two weeks, pops fucked up big time," we were sitting in Paradise chilling.

"Excuse me my name is Hayden; I'm looking for the boss of this cub?" Some thick ass bitch said while standing in front of us.

"What's up?" I asked not really paying attention to her.

"I'm looking for a job," She whispered. I noticed that she kept fidgeting with her fingers and looking behind her.

"Nope," Staci said answering for me while sitting on my lap.

"You heard my lady ma," I replied trying not to get on her bad side.

"Hey, my name is Kenyon, I'm part owner of the establishment. I can't hire you as a dancer, but I can hire you as my brother's assistant is that coo?" Kenyon asked trying to sound professional.

"Yes that's fine, when do I start?" She asked with a smile on her face.

"Didn't I say no!" Staci yelled causing Kenyon to laugh and ignore her.

"This is my brother Carter, you will be helping him," Kenyon replied. She smile and wave at Carter, but his rude ass just nodded and walked away.

"You can start tomorrow and don't be late," Carter said.

"Bye," Ashton said waving her off. She's been around longer than Staci, so she already peeped game. Even though Carter and Ash are no longer together they decided to at least be cordial for Pooh.

"I told yall niggas it's been too quiet," I said while taking a pull from the blunt.

"What's up bitches," Davon greeted while walking in our section with Killa and Toy behind him.

"Who are you texting Toy?" Ash said trying to be nosey.

"Damn, Carter I mean Davon get yo nosey ass girl," Toy said causing Kenyon to start laughing at her petty ass.

"So Vonna's birthday is next month, and I wanted to take her to Disney World," Killa said smiling trying to change the subject.

"I'm down," Kenyon said.

"Count me in," Ash said as well.

"So, everybody agree?"

"Agree with what?" Pooh said while walking in.

"Kayin!" Pooh screamed and jumped on Kayin's lap.

"Pooh get yo big ass off of me," Kayin laughed while tickling her.

"Stop Kayin," She laughed and got up. She ran to Kenyon and jumped on his back.

"Pooh get yo silly ass off of me," Kenyon said while smiling hard.

"No tell me you miss me." She started kissing his face.

"Okay okay, I miss you shit." she got down and just looked at me.

"Hi Kj" she said and walked away trying to act like she was mad, but I already knew what was about to happen.

"Ka'Mari!" Pooh cried and ran towards and jumped on me, we both fell on the floor and busted out laughing.

"I missed you too pooh," I admitted before kissing her cheek, we both got up and she went to sit on Killa's lap.

"So what was yall talking about?" Pooh said.

"Man get yo nosey ass on," Kenyon said, she just laughed and started talking to the girls.

"So, did pops find any leads on this God nigga?" I asked.

"Man nah he haven't, he said he couldn't trace that number at all," Killa said.

"Some shit ain't adding up with that though. I think Ahmad was teaming up with somebody on the inside." Kayin said.

"You think we got a snake on our team?" Carter asked sounding shocked.

"I mean it's possible, this shit feels close to home, almost like its personal," Kayin said.

"True cause they ain't fucking with nobody except for Kj and Pooh. Ever since we killed Ahmad our business had been running smooth, shit seems kind of weird to me," Davon said

"Yea that shit don't sound right, either God is one weird mother fucking, or he has it out for yall," Carter said. I looked at Pooh and she was just staring at me with a blank expression, she obviously heard the conversation that was going on.

"Well whatever happens, I'm down with yall," Davon said while rolling up a blunt.

"Shit it's whatever to me, at this point I'm ready to paint the whole city red, I don't play when it comes to my family," I said, I'm tired of waiting on pops to do something about the situation, it's time to do shit my way.

CHAPTER 23

Pooh

"Lord I can't be pregnant," I cried while looking the pregnancy test that said positive clear as day.

"What am I going to do with another baby I can't do this alone," I cried while quickly picking up my phone and called

Ash.

"Hello?"

"Hey Ash, are you busy"

"Not really, are you okay?"

"No can you come over?"

"I'm on my way," She said before hanging up the phone, our friendship is not as strong as it used to be, but I really needed her right now.

2 weeks ago

Devin was knocked out on the couch for the third day this week, he has been coming in late every day for the past two months.

"Good morning mommy!" Vonna said while walking in the kitchen.

"Goodmorning baby," I kissed her face and sat her back down. Dev's phone kept

ringing irritating my life, so I answered it.

"Hello?"

"Hello is Devin there?" Some bitch asked.

"Um he's sleep, who's calling?"

"My name is Hayden; I was just making sure he made it home safe," I could tell that she was being petty, but I wasn't going to let her get to me.

"Oh, let me wake him up for you sweetie," shot back while walking in the living room and standing over him debating if I

wanted to end his cheating ass life.

"Devin wake up"

"What Bianca damn," Thats another thing he did, I was no longer *"Bae, baby, B, or Mama"* I was *"Bianca"*

"Hayden's on the phone, she wants to know of you made it home safe." I responded, he got up and snatched his phone from me. I just walked back in the kitchen while laughing.

"Mommy what's wrong, you're crying," Vonna said while wrapping her arms around me.

"Nothing baby, go get ready for school," I said. After I finished cleaning up the kitchen, I went upstairs to find Devin.

"Who is this Hayden bitch who got you forgetting that you have a family at home?" I asked while looking at him, but he was too busy in his phone.

"I met her at the club two months ago," he answered un-interested in the conversation.

"Well obviously you're feeling her, because she got you turning your back on your family, are you fucking her?" I cried, he got up and tried to touch me but I quickly snatched away.

"Baby I'm sorry."

"No don't say that, Kj told me that you are no good but like a dumb ass I didn't believe him, I HATE YOU!"

Present day

"Babe what's wrong?" Ash asked while getting in bed with Staci right behind her.

"Devin is cheating on me, what did I do wrong y'all, I thought we were happy" I cried. "What did I do wrong yall"

"Oh, hell no, this nigga got us fucked up, where the fuck my gun at" Staci said while getting up.

"You didn't do anything wrong baby don't beat yourself up for this," Ash said ignoring Staci's crazy ass.

"I'm pregnant," I blurted out while crying harder, they both screamed and started jumping on the bed, unable to control myself, I started laughing.

"Can yall sit down?" I yelled, Ash looked at her phone and frowned.

"I gotta go yall mommy duties!" She kissed me then walked out.

"Stac I think I want to get an abortion," I whispered as soon as Ash walked out.

"Oh baby fuck no, you will not abort my baby because Killa ain't shit, I am the God mother right," I just laughed and nodded.

"You know I don't fuck with Ash like that Stac" Staci and I became close over these past couple of months and now we were inseparable.

"Bitch get up and get cute, we are about to go shopping on Kj!" Staci said while standing up in the bed and twerking, I just laughed and got up, what would I do without my best friend in my life.

. . . .

"Girl Kj has been going crazy cause you ain't talking to him," Staci said with a chuckle. I rolled my eyes and picked my fork up, Kj knew that Dev was cheating on me, but he said that he had to stick to the "Bro code." As soon as I was about to put my rice in my mouth somebody smacked it out of my hand.

"Why the fuck are you feeding my seed that shit Bianca?" I turned around and Devin was behind me with a frown on his face, when I looked to his left and Hayden was standing by his side smiling like something was funny.

"Aw hell nah nigga you got me fucked up, standing over there with Chicken Little. Bitch you look like a fucking chicken." I busted out laughing at Staci's crazy ass.

"Come on let's go Stac his ass is not worth it" I said while walking away, truth be told I didn't want him to see me crying.

"How did he find out you're pregnant?" Stac asked.

"Probably Ash" I shrugged.

"Well let's pop up on that ass, dumb ass bitch gone sell us out when we're supposed to be her sisters," she said getting hyped.

"Nah I just want to go home; I'm probably going to end up at Carter's house any ways."

"Well you do that; I'm going to go pop up on Ash and pray that I won't have to beat her up." She said then got in the car. I'm so happy I decided to give our friendship a try, I know for a fact she would ride for me until the wheels fall off.

• •

"Carter where yo yellow ass at, and that bitch Tiffany better not be in here either!" I screamed while walking in the door.

"Kayin how the fuck am I supposed to tell her that?" I heard Carter said on the phone. I stood behind the door trying to hear what he was talking about. I had a feeling his ass was keeping something from me because of how distant he's been.

"Man just tell her, she's going to start noticing that you are being distance, and not trying to be around her, you know she is going to ask you about it."

"Kayin you don't get what I'm saying bro, how the fuck am I going to tell Bianca that I'm feeling her, she is engaged to Killa, did you forget that," not being able to take it anymore I walked in the room and made myself known.

"Carter what are you talking about?" I asked, he turned around and just stared at me.

"Well that's one way to tell her, I'll let yall talk." Kayin said then hung up.

"Carter what's going on?"

"Just leave it alone Bianca!" He yelled sounding frustrated before running his hands across his face.

"CARTER STOP FUCKING PLAYING WITH ME!" I yelled right back. He sighed and just looked at me.

"I'm feeling you Bianca, I can't get you outta my mind, all I think about is you, your smile, laugh, the way you play with your hair and fingers when you're nervous, the way you shake when you're mad. I can't even fuck my girl cause I'm thinking about how yo pussy would feel around my dick, how soft your lips are, I wanna know how it would feel to wake up next to you every morning, this shit is fucked up Pooh." He was leaning on the wall biting his lip. I wiped the tear that was falling and walked over to him. I wrapped my arms around his waist and looked up at him.

"Carter look at me, I love you, God knows I do, but I'm not the girl for you, Tiffany is, she is an amazing woman and she loved you with all her heart, if I need to fall back I will even though...." He laughed then looked away.

"Carter stop acting like a kid," I warned. He pulled my arms off of him and went to sit on the chair that was in his room.

"Pooh you don't understand," I walked over to him and sat on his lap.

"All those feelings you have, I do too, Carter I think about you all the time, but I know I can't have you because it's wrong. I tried hard to fight these feelings, but I can't, I'm in love Dev and you're feeling Tiffany. Carter, I got feelings for you too but can't lose my bestfriend." I never wanted him to find out, I've always had feelings for Carter I just didn't wanna act on them.

"How long have you been feeling me Bianca?" He asked sounding shocked.

"Since we first met," I whispered while putting my head down

"Really Bianca, you could've fucking told me!" He yelled causing me to jump.

"I know."

"Well why didn't you tell me?"

Because I heard you talking about me to yo friends, Carter you called me fat," he pushed me off of him and got up.

"So, you started fucking with Ahmad, my fucking best friend?"

"I'm sorry Carter," that was the only thing I could get out because I knew that he was mad. He walked towards me and kissed me, I should've pulled away, but I didn't instead I kissed him back.

"Let me have you just for tonight," He laid me down and took my close off.

"Carter," I moaned as he started sucking on my clit and playing with my pussy.

"Shit carter I can't take it please stop," I cried while grabbing his head pushing him deeper in between my legs.

"I'm about to cum!" I screamed

"Cum for daddy Pooh," ss soon as she said that I came all over his face.

"Turn that ass around, I'm not done with you," I turned around and arched my back as he slid halfway in then stopped.

"Fuck Pooh that pussy gripping my dick," He groaned while easing inside of me.

"Mmmm shit," I moaned while throwing it back as soon as I adjusted to his size.

"Fuck yo shit so wet," He started going faster causing my eyes to roll in the back of my head deeper and my eyes rolled in the back of my head.

"Oh my god Carter I'm about to cum!"

"Cum with Daddy Pooh," he reached forward and started playing with my clit.

"FUCK!" He grunted as we came together.

"Fuck we forgot to use a condom," He said while laughing, I looked at him already know he was about to flip out.

"Um I'm pregnant," I whispered

"What the fuck Bianca are you serious, I just fucked you, and you got another nigga's seeds in you." He screamed.

"Carter I'm sorry I was just caught up in the moment."

"Whatever dude I'm about to shower," He said then walked away, I knew better than to go after his as when he was mad, so I just laid there and fell asleep cause this nigga just wore me out.

• •

"Pooh get up and get yo phone," I opened my eyes and Carter was up watching tv and drinking coffee.

"Hello."

"Wassup B," When I heard Dev's voice, I rolled my eyes.

"Hi Devin, what do you want?"

"Where are my kids?" He asked probably trying to hold a conversation.

"With yo daddy waiting on you." I said then hung up and snatched Carter's coffee out of his hand.

"Get the fuck out." He barked which caused me to laugh.

"Awww are you mad big baby?' I joked while pinching his cheek.

"You wake up and start playing."

"Carter where yo bitch ass at?" I heard Kj yelled while walking up the stairs.

"Oh shit, I forgot I told him to come over" Carter whispered in a panic.

"Will you chill yo paranoid ass out." I laughed.

"Please tell me yall didn't do what I think y'all did" Kj stressed while walking in.

"Yea they did, this bitch walking around all happy and shit." Ash said while walking in causing me to start laughing on accident cause I knew that she was pissed.

"Ash..." Carter said feeling bad, but I honestly could care less.

"Shut up Carter, so you fucked my man Pooh, that's how we doing it now?" I looked at her then started laughing even harder.

"Bitch Carter is not your man anymore, Davon is, yes I fucked Carter so what didn't you fuck Ahmad and have a baby by him?" I asked but instead of responding she just walked out. Kj grabbed the blunt off the dresser and shook his head.

"Yo I'll be back in a second cause yall are tripping, Carter be ready when I get back please." Kj said then walked out. I laid back down and laid my head on his lap.

"You know you pissed her off right?" Carter said.

"I don't give a fuck, what is she mad for?"

"Cause I gave you some of this dick." He whispered in my ear.

"Nigga it wasn't all that anyways." I lied while getting up and running, he grabbed me from behind and pinned my arms behind my back and started tickling me.

"Say sorry"

"Carter stop, you gone make me pee on myself, okay okay sorry," I whined, whe let me go and ran and jumped on his back, threw me on the bed and bit me hard.

"Owe Carter that hurt" I pouted. He kissed my arm then laid down.

"You are so spoiled." He said while pulling me on him.

"You, Kj, and daddy got me this way."

"Kenyon and Kayin do too," He started playing in my hair which instantly caused me to drift off.

"How did we end up here?" He blurted out.

"What do you mean Carter?"

"I mean it feels right don't it?" He looked down at me and kissed my forehead. I smiled nodded my head, it did feel right, I just wasn't ready for a relationship.

"Let's give it a try, fuck what everybody got too say."

"Can we just take things slow, I'm not ready for another relationship." I explained.

"Anything you want baby," he kissed my lips, and played with my hair until I fell asleep. I know a lot people are going to say something, but at this point I honestly didn't care, it was about what it going to make me happy, and right now its Carter.

CHAPTER 24

Kj

"Yo ass better be dressed nigga!" I yelled walking up the stairs.

"What's up nigga," He greeted never taking his eyes of the tv, I sat on the couch in his room and just looked at him. Pooh was in his bed with her head in his lap sleep, while he smoked a blunt. This is some weird shit, and I already know that Killa's ass is going to have a fit when he finds out.

"Yo, I'm not even gone ask, but we need to roll out, we got an emergency meeting" He nodded and sat his blunt down.

"Pooh wake up baby girl," he whispered gently shaking her.

"Carter please stop talking to me," she said while trying to fall back asleep

"I'm about to go with your brother's ma, text me when you wake up." She lifted her head up, then puckered her lips, when he bent down to kiss her, I just shook my head.

"Aw hell nah, my sister is smashing the homie!" Kenyon

said. Pooh busted out laughing and got out of the bed, I'm glad she had clothes on.

"Hey yall!" She kissed our cheeks then wrapped her arms around Carter.

"When are you coming back?"

"I don't know ma why?" He asked looking all in love and shit.

"Can you bring me back a subway sandwich?"

"Yea now moved so I can go" He kissed her lips then walked out. This is a problem waiting to happen I can already tell.

• •

"So, where the fuck is our shipment Unc?" Killa ask our connect while taking a pull from his blunt. Our shipment has been coming up missing for the past couple of weeks and we are tired of it.

"Little nigga we've been delivering yall shipment on time, that little nigga Quese comes to pick it up."

"Please don't tell me this nigga has been stealing our shit!" I yelled while banging my fist on the table.

"I'm tired of this shit man!" Kayin roared with nothing but murder in his eyes. As soon as I was about to reason, my business phone started ringing.

"Yea" I answered without looking at the caller id.

"You got a snake on your team son"

"What the fuck you mean pops!" I shot back.

"Aye watch yo fucking mouth talking to me like that, listen and don't say shit to anybody."

"Alright"

"Somebody went to Paradise and cleaned out the safe, when we checked the Cameras they were turned off, they also went to all of y'all traps and killed some of your strongest men. Word on the street is that they have a hit on your team including Pooh, whoever this is calls himself God, and use to work with Ahmad," he explained.

"Fuck man, alright pops."

"Tell your brother's and that's it," I hung up and threw my phone against the wall.

"You good bro?" Kayin asked.

"Nah, Kenyon, Kayin, and Carter follow me," As soon as we stepped outside I told them what pops said.

"Fuck this can't be happening right now, yall think it's one of our boys? Carter asked referring to Killa and Davon.

"Nah I can't even see them setting us up, they our brothers' man." I answered.

"Well whoever this is calls himself God," Kayin said.

"Well God is in for a rude awakening," I said.

"Pops want us to meet him at his warehouse," Kayin said reading a text from his phone.

"I'll go get the Killa and Davon," Kenyon said while running back inside, I quickly got in my car and called Rock.

"What's up Bro."

"Aye do me a favor go get the kids, and women and take them to the hide out spot."

"Bet, anything else bro?"

"Yea when you're done meet us at Pops house, we may need you to come out of retirement." I answered truthfully

"Say no more bro, you know my trigger finger stay ready." He said then hung up. When I started the car Kayin hopped in and pulled a blunt out of his pocket.

"Bro are you good?" He asked while taking a pull from the blunt.

"Yea I just hope that I don't have to kill any of my brothers' man," he leaned back in deep thought. I really hope that I won't have to kill anybody close to me.
• •

"What's going on pops?" I said as soon as I walked in.

"Now that everyone is here, I can show yall why I brought yall here." My pops said with no expression. I looked at my Unc and he had the same exact expression on his face.

"So, what the fuck are we here for pops?" Kenyon's impatient ass asked.

"Who was in charge of killing Ahmad?" Uncle D asked.

"We all had a part in it," I said. My pops nodded and opened the doors to the warehouse.

"YO WHAT THE FUCK IS GOING ON, I KILLED THIS DUDE!" Carter yelled.

"Carter man you was slipping son, you let yo emotions get the best of you and aimed for his chest instead of his head son," My pops explained, I couldn't even say anything cause I was too busy looking at Ahmad who was actually alive, my father had him tide to a chair.

"What's up brothers, long time no see," Ahmad said with a devilish grin on his face. The fact that he was still alive brought back memories of all the bullshit he put my sister through, and without any hesitation I pulled out my gun and emptied the clip in him making sure to get all head shots, Kenyon, Kayin, and Carter all did the same showing no remorse.

"Well he's dead now, is that all you needed pops?" I said clearly uninterested in having a conversation with him.

"No that's not all I need, If yall wouldn't of waited to get our help all of this shit could've been avoided, but instead yall decided to try to kill Ahmad off of emotion which you shouldn't do at all, yall are acting like boys instead of men!" He yelled. I laughed and pinched the bridge of my nose trying to calm myself down.

"Pop you act like you got room to talk, instead up taking care of your responsibilities and owning up to the fact that you fucked up, you decided to give your daughter away but you're a man, get the fuck outta here, at the end of the day this shit is done, Ahmad is gone, and we can go back to living our normal lives," I said then stormed off, I don't have to listen to a man who can even own up to the fact that he fucked up.

CHAPTER 25

God

"I can't believe they killed my fucking brother, Quese where the fuck was yo ass at when they found him!" I yelled while pacing back and forth.

The only family I had left is gone all because of me.

"I'm sorry boss, I was picking up the shipment."

"Get the fuck outta here while you're still breathing my nigga," He quickly got up and left. I picked up my ringing phone and answered it without looking at the id.

"Yea."

"Boss nobody is at Killa's shop except for that bitch Toy," one of my workers responded.

"Good looking out bro," I said then hung up. These niggas are about to feel me for killing my brother.
• •

"Bitch hurry yo slow ass up before I beat yo ass!" I said while pointing the gun at Toy's stupid ass.

"Nigga fuck you, I ain't giving yo ass shit, you gone have to kill me!" I pulled the trigger and walked out, that bitch talks to much, plus I never liked her gay ass anyway.

"What's up Quese?" I said as I answered the phone.

"We are all set boss, we got the girl, what do you want us to do with them?"

"Tie them to a chair, I got a plan" I laughed. I can't wait until I take over, it's time to shut these niggas up for good. They killed my brother and I'm about to hit them where it hurts... Bianca

CHAPTER 26

Pooh

"**I**f yall don't stop fucking crying I'm gone beat yall ass!" I yelled getting irritated. Staci and Ashton have been crying since we been here, and it's pissing me off, that is not going to help the situation we are in. I was mad cause I got caught slipping, now a bitch all kidnapped and shit. I heard the guy who Kidnapped us on the phone with some nigga name God, as I listened to God's it sounded very familiar to me, I just couldn't figure out who it belonged to.

"Bitch they got us tied up" Ashton cried.

"Oh my gosh please shut the fuck up stating the obvious Ash," I shot back while rubbing my temples.

"Aye bitch, shut the fuck up," he said.

"Fuck you pussy, you better hope Kj kill you before I do, wait no I hope he kill yo mama first," I was trying to get a reaction out of him, dumb ass didn't tie me up tight enough so I managed to get out. When he ran towards me, I grabbed his gun and shot him right between the eyes.

" Ahh fuck, where did you learn to shoot like that?" Staci asked.

"Bitch I'm the daughter of two savages, and my biological father Ka'Mari runs this city, it would be disrespectful if I didn't know how to bust a gun." I explained, all of a sudden the door opened and this big nigga walked in.

"How the fuck..." he didn't have time to finish his sentence I shot him, we ran out of the house and called Kj.

"What the fuck is going on Ka'Mari, these weak ass niggas just tried to kidnap us!" I wasn't trying to yell at him, but I was just too pissed off.

"Bianca what the fuck are you talking about?"

"Nigga that God had somebody kidnap us!" I yelled getting irritated.

"Come to the house now, where are the kids?" He asked in a panic.

"With Devin's mama" I said before hanging up the phone. Since we were kidnapped, we had to get in an UBER which was another thing I was pissed about. When we made it to the house everybody was there looking pissed. I guessed Devin expected me to come running to him but that was not going to happen. When I walked over to Carter and stood in between his legs Devin looked at me with a murderous look. This is not how I wanted him to find out about me and Carter, but oh well. Ash and Staci ran to their men and cried, I couldn't even cry I was pissed.

"Carter can you take me home please?" I asked while laying my head on his chest.

"No, you don't need to be alone, you're staying at Carter's house," Kj said.

"That's fine, come on Carter damn, I'm hungry!"

"Can she stay with yall?" Carter asked while grabbing me by my waist and kissing my neck. I   couldn't help but feel bad when I looked at Devin, I know it's hard to see me with somebody else.

"Hell nah" everybody said at the same time.

"Fuck all yall pussies!" I laughed while flipping them off and getting in the car. When we made it to the house, I couldn't get out the car fast enough. Ever since we left Kj's house, Carter has been going on non-stop asking me if I'm okay and what happened.

"Carter leave me alone damn, I said I'm fine," I yelled

"You know what fuck it, I'm tryna make sure yo ass is okay, do you know how fucked up I felt when Kj told me somebody kidnapped you, I could've lost yo stupid ass!" He punched a hole in the wall and walked away. I didn't realize that I was being selfish until now, I found him on the balcony smoking a blunt, so I wrapped my arms around him and laid my head on his back.

"I'm sorry daddy, I didn't mean to make you mad," I whispered, he turned around and looked at me.

"I thought I lost you ma," I smiled and kissed his lips.

"But you didn't, I love you baby,"

"I love you too, ow watch out so I can go get our food," he kissed me then walked away.
• •

I was sleeping good as shit until some told me to wake up, and as soon as I opened my I noticed some mask men standing over me, but before I could react one of them put a towel over my mouth, and I was out like a light.

"Damn God it's been three hours, how long is she going to sleep?" My eyes fluttered opened to the sounds of voiced, that's when I realized that I was in a basement tied to a chair... Again.

"Well Hello Sleeping Beauty!" I was staring at these bitches, Hayden and Tiffany.

"Are you shocked to see us?" Hayden asked with a smirk on her face.

"Bitch you ain't shit without that gun," I shot back not scared of them, Tiffany looked at Hayden and smirked, they both walked over to me and started kicking my ass.

"Aye chill that's enough!" I heard somebody bark, I could barely move, both of my eyes were swollen, and I could barely breathe, but they wasn't going to see not one tear fall out my eye. The man who told them to stop sat directly in front of me wearing a mask like some bitch ass nigga.

"So you're God?" I asked while spitting blood on his shoes. He picked my chair up and forced me to look at him.

"Bitch I've been waiting a long time for this," he laughed. These bitches must have beat me senseless cause there was no way I was hearing his voice right now; he couldn't be God.

"Oh lord please tell me I'm hearing shit," I said out loud hoping that it was a dream.

"Nah baby girl, you ain't it's really me."

"Carter?" I said barely above a whisper trying to fight back the tears.

"Nah best friend, its God," he took his mask off and smirked......

TO BE CONTINUED............

Made in the USA
Middletown, DE
12 November 2023

42398827R00109